LEGENDS

O F T H E

FERENGI™

By Quark as told to
Ira Steven Behr and
Robert Hewitt Wolfe

POCKET BOOKS

New York   London   Toronto   Sydney   Tokyo   Singapore

An *Original* Publication of POCKET BOOKS

POCKET BOOKS, a division of Simon & Schuster Inc.
1230 Avenue of the Americas, New York, NY 10020

ISBN: 0-671-00728-9

First Pocket Books trade paperback printing August 1997

10   9   8   7   6   5   4   3   2   1

POCKET and colophon are registered trademarks of Simon & Schuster Inc.

Book design by Richard Oriolo

Printed in the U.S.A.

For orders other than by individual consumers, Pocket Books grants a discount of **10 or more copies** of single titles for special markets or premium use. For further details, please write to the Vice-President of Special Markets, Pocket Books, 1633 Broadway, New York, NY 10019-6785 8th Floor.

For information on how individual consumers can place orders, please write to Mail Order Department, Simon & Schuster, Inc. 200 Old Tappan Road, Old Tappan, NJ 07675.

INTRODUCTION

Let's get one thing clear. My esteemed publisher paid me to write a book. Which I did.

Okay, okay. Actually, I didn't write a word of it. I jobbed it out to a couple of fathead hew-mons named Behr and Wolfe. (Behr and Wolfe? What are they? Writers, or creatures of the forest?)

But the point is, no one got paid to write an introduction. *That* my publisher wants for free. And now Wolfe and Behr have scurried off, back to their dens or lairs or wherever they live, and I have to write this myself. Life is so unfair.

Anyway, here it is——the introduction, everything you need to know about this book.

FERENGI

Natives of the planet Ferenginar. A short, wily, magnificently lobed spacefaring people. Numerous pictures of these handsome folk can be found throughout this volume.

RULES OF ACQUISITION

"The two hundred and eighty-five guiding principles that form the basis of Ferengi business philosophy." (A direct quote from my previous book *The Ferengi Rules of Acquisition* by Quark as told to Ira Steven Behr. Still available in a bookstore near you!)

LEGENDS OF THE FERENGI

"A collection of stories, fables, folk songs, philosophical meditations, and outright lies based on the Ferengi Rules of Acquisition." Just like it says on the cover.

Well, there you go. The introduction. I hope you liked it. Now on to the good stuff.

I really hate working for free.

Quark, Son of Keldar
Proprietor
Quark's Bar, Grill, Gaming House, and Holosuite Arcade,
a wholly owned subsidiary of Quark Enterprises, Inc.

The first two words any Ferengi (Armin Shimerman) learns
in the hew-mon language: "no refunds."

RULE
#

In the village of Noi, there once lived a shopkeeper named Obe. Though his shop was small, he was well known for his many eccentricities. Chief among them was his insistence on "honesty" in all things. His goods were of the finest quality, his prices were fair and reasonable, and his weighing scales were accurate to one one-thousandth of a milliyop. He was, needless to say, the least popular man in the village.

One morning, Obe was seated behind the counter when a customer entered. This was quite an event, since no one in Noi would shop at the store of such an obvious lunatic. The new customer, Greb, a weary traveller headed for his home in the distant village of Korpa, purchased a single canister of beetle snuff and then hurried on. It was a full hour later before Obe realized that Greb had overpaid him by a half slip of latinum. Wracked with guilt, Obe set out for Korpa, determined to make restitution. But he was never to reach his destination.

Halfway to Korpa, Obe was set upon and brutally murdered by assassins hired by none other than Greb. It seems the man from Korpa had been carrying on a secret affair with Obe's wife. Shortly after the funeral, Greb moved into Obe's house, married his wife, and took over his store, where he made a fortune over-charging his customers for inferior merchandise.

Legend has it that the townspeople of Noi, wanting to make an example of Obe's foolishness, decided to bury the shopkeeper with the half strip of latinum he had so desperately wanted to return. Unfortunately, someone (probably Greb) stole the latinum out of his hand during the funeral.

From the sad tale of Obe came the First Rule of Acquisition:

*"Once you have their money, you
never give it back."*

Ira Steven Behr and Robert Hewitt Wolfe

R U L E
#3

Back in the early days (and by this we mean the real early early early days, not just olden times, or a while ago) when Ferenginar was young and green (and it didn't rain so much), there were two races vying for control of the planet's surface. One was the Ferengi, and the other was the Gree. Back then, the Ferengi were possessed of a tall, dark beauty, with magnificent feathered crests and long supple tails. Their striking good looks were the envy of all other creatures.

The Gree, on the other hand, were towering giants with long horny claws, poison-tipped barbs instead of hair, and seven rows of razor-sharp teeth. The wars between the Ferengi and the Gree were fierce, bloody, and without profit. Finally, the Blessed Exchequer tired of the bloodshed and descended unto Ferenginar from the Divine Treasury. Gathering together the leaders of the Ferengi and the Gree, He offered a peaceful solution to their conflict. He would hold a Sacred Auction. The prize: the Divine Right to rule Ferenginar. Each race would bid their proudest attributes, sacrificing them in exchange for mastery of the world.

The Gree opened the auction by bidding their poison-tipped barbs, which were duly collected by the Blessed Exchequer. The Ferengi countered by offering their luxuriant pelts, which were made into fur coats for wives of the Celestial Auctioneers. The Gree threw in their horny claws. The Ferengi upped the ante with their feathered crests. The Gree bid their legs, the Ferengi their tails. This spirited bidding continued until the Ferengi had also traded away their height, their straight teeth, and their perfect complexions, leaving them looking very much like they do today . . . hairless, compact, and bright orange.

Finally, in a final desperate bid to defeat their competition, the Gree gave away everything that made them what they were . . . their four arms, their farseeing eyes, their gigantic size. The Exchequer made them the masters of the world, and in exchange they became small worm-like creatures, their now-tiny razor-sharp teeth fit only for burrowing in the soil. The Ferengi had lost.

4

When it comes to doing business with another species
(Randy Oglesby), Ferengi always take care to get
the upper hand.

Or had they? For as soon as the auction was over, Ferengi
the world over began trapping the now-helpless little Gree and
proceeded to eat them. For a few short days, the Gree had
bought themselves the right to be masters of the world, but at
what price? Without their enormous size, their barbs, their
claws, their arms, and their legs, the Gree were soon reduced to
a succulent snack.

Hence the Third Rule of Acquisition:

"Never pay more for an Acquisition than you have to."

R U L E
6

When DaiMon Greko was only a little bitty Ferengi, his father began to fear he had some Klingon blood in him (on his mother's side, of course). Young Greko was a fierce, aggressive, and physically fearless lobeling, not at all like the conniving, calculating, and devious normal Ferengi children he grew up with. But as it turned out, Greko's father had no need for concern. For shortly after the lad grew to adulthood, the Ferengi purchased warp drive (at a substantial discount) from the Breen, and Greko found his niche in life. He became DaiMon Greko, the most famous (and most highly paid) ship's captain of his time.

Needless to say, Greko's father was delighted and sent his three other sons, Mecko, Hecko, and Trop, to serve under Greko. Greko found the arrangement to his liking. He was quite fond of his brothers, and his crew often said that with their appearance aboard ship, Greko finally learned to enjoy the fruits of his labor. The four brothers would stay up all night playing tongo, listening to aural sculpture, and sharing Orion slave girls in Greko's holosuite. Yes, they were indeed a happy band of brothers.

Then one day, while the ship was carrying a load of top quality beetle snuff back to Ferenginar, Mecko, Hecko, and Trop decided to run a high-stakes game of three-toss in the cargo bay. In the middle of the game, the ship hit a freak warp eddy. The cargo bay was breached, and in danger of being decompressed into space.

Greko had to think fast. He could either save his beloved brothers by employing the emergency transporters to beam them to safety, or use the transporters to beam away the beetle snuff (estimated value three hundred bars of latinum). He couldn't save both. Greko had to decide between the lives of his brothers and a sizable profit. It was not an easy decision. But Greko knew what he had to do.

Sure, they may behave like your average, well-adjusted Ferengi family (Aron Eisenberg, Armin Shimerman, Max Grodénchik) . . . but only if the latinum is right.

With the latinum he earned from the beetle snuff, Greko built three life-sized statues of his dearly departed brothers and placed them in the garden of his ancestral home. They can still be seen there today (for a small admission fee).

DaiMon Greko never forgot the Sixth Rule of Acquisition:

"Never allow family to stand in the way of opportunity."

Learn from the example of Grand Nagus Zek (Wallace
Shawn): always grab the bull by the lobes.

RULE
#7

I t is a well known fact that the most popular personal groom-
ing accessory for Ferengi males over the age of a hundred
and fifty is Gweemo's Lobemaster, "The Hair-Trimmer for
Distinguished Ferengi." But few know that the Lobemaster did
not catch on in its initial release. Gweemo himself almost went
bankrupt. But then his nephew, Squim, came up with the slogan,
"Keep Your Ears Open. Use Gweemo's Lobemaster."

Needless to say, the new marketing plan was a brilliant
success. In fact, it was the single most successful advertising
campaign in the history of Ferenginar. That, combined with the
fact that Lobemasters were given away for free but replacement
bladeheads cost eighteen strips of latinum apiece, soon made
Gweemo and Squim rich beyond their wildest dreams.

In honor of their unprecedented success, Grand Nagus Drik
(for a sizable compensation) arranged it so that all Ferengi
would remember their slogan forever.

So practice the Seventh Rule of Acquisition:Get a Gweemo's
Lobemaster and

"Keep Your Ears Open!"

Would-be entrepreneurs, don't make this mistake. Never let *anybody* read you *anything*. That includes this book. Buy your own copy. Buy two copies. Oh, frinx, just order a case and be done with it.

RULE
#8

By purchasing a copy of the book, *The Legends of the Ferengi*, henceforth known as "The Book," the buyer, henceforth known as "The Mark," agrees to all of the following conditions: He, she, or it will render unto the authors of The Book all earnings accrued during the rest of this century, unless the turn of the century occurs in less than five years, in which case The Mark will continue to surrender all capital gains for the next twenty-five years. The Mark will also immediately surrender any and all baseball cards in their possession containing the likeness, be it photo or artist's rendering, of Mickey Charles Mantle, a.k.a. the Mick, a.k.a. the Commerce Comet, a.k.a., the Greatest Switch-hitter in the History of Baseball. Finally, the Mark also agrees to forfeit the sum total of their personal collection of naked photos, holograms, or holosuite images of Demi Moore, Sharon Stone, Drew Barrymore (over the age of eighteen), Cameron Diaz, Claudia Schiffer, Elle MacPherson, Jennifer McCarthy, Naomi Campbell, or any other person who has been described in the press with any of the following labels: "sex personified," "a hot-looking babe," OR "the nineties 'It' Girl." Please do not send pictures of Pamela Anderson Lee, whose naked photos have been published *ad nauseam* here on Ferenginar and no longer have any appreciable market value.

This should help you to remember the Eighth Rule of Acquisition:

"Small print leads to large risk."

Ira Steven Behr and Robert Hewitt Wolfe

RULE
#9

ollowing is an excerpt from the personal ledger of Grand
Nagus Frek, the pioneer of Ferengi Econosolipsistic
Mathematics:

This is the first ever appearance of the Ninth Rule of
Acquisition:

"Opportunity plus instinct equals profit."

12

As the hew-mons would say: "Eureka!"

Avarice never dies. And if it's really lucky,
it gets to be Nagus.

RULE
#10

When the Scribes of the Sacred Illuminated Balance Sheet were about to put out their commemorative one thousandth edition, they approached Grand Nagus Brolok and asked him to provide a parable for the Tenth Rule of Acquisition. Brolok pocketed the customary bribe, thought for a moment, and then spoke the following words of wisdom:

"Some rules need no explanation."

By taking the amount of the Scribes' bribe and calculating it out on a per-word basis, this observation earned Brolok the distinction of uttering the most expensive words in Ferengi history.

This demonstrated Brolok's complete mastery of the Tenth Rule of Acquisition:

"Greed is Eternal."

Risk and profit go hand in hand.

RULE
13

Things worth doing for money:	Things not worth doing for money:
Jump up and down on one foot until your hipbone is pounded into dust.	
Lie to your boss.	
Tell your boss the truth.	
Help rich old Ferengi across the street.	
Shove rich old Ferengi into traffic.	
Show respect to your elders.	
Three words: Professional Food Taster	
Sell people ground-up beetles and convince them to snort them up their noses.	
Stick stuff in your ears.	
Stick stuff in other people's ears.	
Create your own religion.	
Spread vicious rumors about your enemies.	
Spread vicious rumors about your friends.	
Spread vicious rumors about yourself.	
Blame the innocent.	
Practice the One Hundred and Thirteenth Rule of Acquisition. (Go ahead. Look it up.)	
Hang out with Klingons.	
Write silly stories about people in the distant future.	

Never forget the Thirteenth Rule of Acquisition:
"Anything worth doing is worth doing for money."

R U L E
16

The following is a standard rider attached to any quotation of the Sixteenth Rule of Acquisition:

Before reading this rule, raise your right hand to your left lobe and your left hand to your right lobe and recite the following sacred Ferengi oath.

"I, (state your name), do hereby swear to never, under any circumstances, correctly quote this rule to any non-Ferengi. Furthermore, I swear, under penalty of eternal bankruptcy, that even under the most extreme duress, even if a Cardassian is doing unspeakable things to my lobes, I will maintain that the Sixteenth Rule of Acquisition, the most sacred of all Ferengi precepts is . . .

"'A deal is a deal.'

"Period. No further stipulation. No extra clause. That's the rule. Anything else you might've heard is purely rumor."

Thank you. You may now read the Sixteenth Rule of Acquisition:

Which is, of course:

> *"A deal is a deal . . . until a better*
> *one comes along."*

Contrary to what the hew-mons may think, a handshake isn't worth *yamok* sauce. Especially between a Ferengi and a loser like Tiron (Jeffrey Combs).

Have you ever seen two more honest-looking faces?

RULE
# #

The following is a standard rider attached to any quotation of the Seventeenth Rule of Acquisition:

Okay, now wash both hands carefully before proceeding. Then, raise your left hand to your left lobe and your right hand to your right lobe and recite this following sacred Ferengi oath.

We're waiting. Okay, here goes:

"I, (state your name), do hereby swear, to never, under any circumstances, correctly quote this rule to any non-Ferengi. (That's right, this one too.) Furthermore, I swear, under penalty of abstention from oo-mox for as long as I live, that even under extreme duress, even if I'm being force-fed root beer by a demented hew-mon, I will maintain that the Seventeenth Rule of Acquisition, the other most sacred of all Ferengi precepts, is . . .

"'A contract is a contract is a contract.'

"This is the rule we live by. Honest. We promise. Why would we lie? You're bigger and twice as irrationally violent as we are."

Done? Good. That's settled. Now feel free to contemplate the magnificence of the Seventeenth Rule of Acquisition:

Which clearly states:

"A contract is a contract is a contract . . .
but only between Ferengi."

R U L E
#18

Back in the days before Ferenginar purchased warp drive, before the Ferengi became the most important economic power in the known universe, there lived a Ferengi named Frinx. He manufactured the first fully automatic waste extractor (hence the expression, "Excuse me, I have to take a Frinx.") and was a very profitable Ferengi indeed. But one day, Frinx changed. He stopped caring about profit, neglected his business, and spent all his time traveling the planet, doing topographical surveys of its prominent features.

Eventually, this behavior generated suspicion. An intrepid agent of the F.C.A. named Stoonk began investigating Frinx. Eventually Stoonk realized the frightening truth. Frinx was not Frinx. The waste-extraction entrepreneur had been replaced by a hideous alien intelligence bent on the conquest of Ferenginar. The topographical surveys were an excuse to search for suitable landing sites for the invasion fleet.

The alien spy was unmasked in the nick of time. Ferenginar was saved, the false Frinx was held for a sizable ransom, and Stoonk confiscated the waste-extraction business and turned it back into a going concern (hence the expression, "What a Stoonk.").

After his success, the ever-vigilant Stoonk coined the Eighteenth Rule of Acquisition:

"A Ferengi without profit is no Ferengi at all."

If you suspect a phony Ferengi (Ethan Phillips), touch his lobes. If his eyes don't roll up into his head in ecstacy, he's either a ringer, or he's dead.

Please direct any complaints regarding this
publication to somebody else. The author accepts
no responsibility for its content.

RULE
19

Besides being the Nineteenth Rule of Acquisition, the aphorism "Satisfaction is not guaranteed" can be found printed on literally every item manufactured on Ferenginar. Including this one. Right here. So deal with it.

And never forget the Nineteenth Rule of Acquisition:

"Satisfaction is not guaranteed."

R U L E
21

An excerpt from the ancient medical text: *Guarding Your Investment, Keeping Your Children Profitable,* by Doctor Posck, of the Ferengi Wellness Institute:

In our last chapter, we dealt with the problem of excessive, compulsive oo-moxing in male children, ages one to seventeen. Now, we must turn our attention to one of the most stressful events in any young Ferengi's life, the Attainment Ceremony. Parents, relax. Rest assured that the ceremony is largely a formality. When given the choice between spending time with a friend, or receiving a bar of gold-pressed latinum, no Ferengi lad in recent history has passed up the bar. Your son will make the right choice, too. All we suggest is that you make sure that the ceremony is held in a well-lit room, that both the friend and the bar of latinum are equidistant from your child, that the friend is strapped down and gagged to allow an unbiased outcome, and that the bar of latinum is placed at an angle that makes it as shiny as possible.

We highly discourage the use of the Southern Ferenginar version of the Attainment Ceremony. While watching your child and his best friend actually fight over the bar of latinum may be entertaining (and profitable when you run the betting pool), injuries are frequent and can be costly with regard to the long-term growth of your investment.

One final piece of advice. If your child fails the test, DON'T TELL ANYONE! Just bribe everyone present to forget what they've seen and have your son repeat the test as many times as necessary until he gets it right.

Good Luck!

This quote from Posck's centuries-old text (still available for purchase at your local scrollmonger) shows that even from the beginning of Ferengi history, our people knew the fundamental truth of the Twenty-First Rule of Acquisition:

"Never place friendship above profit."

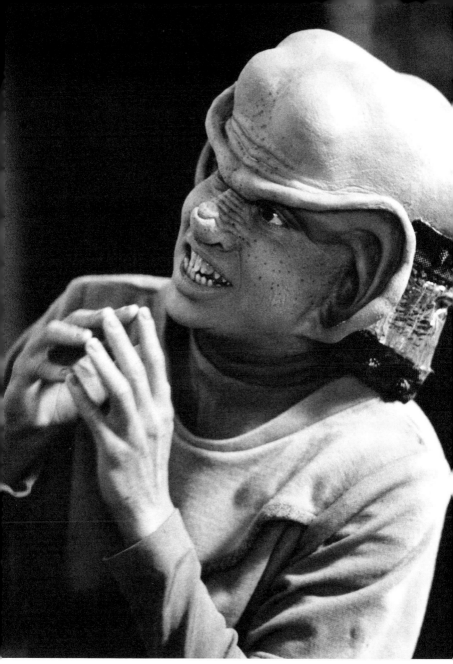

Greed isn't genetic. It has to be learned.
Teach your children well.

R U L E
#22

Back in the dark times of the Barter Age when Ferenginar was divided between tiny warring Commerce Zones, there lived a wandering troubadour named Lonz. A loner owing his commercial loyalty to no one, Lonz travelled the length and breadth of Ferenginar, armed with only his trusty nose flute. It is said that even the participants in the most violent of hostile takeovers would pause to listen to Lonz, known to his fans everywhere as Old Golden Nostril.

By far, his most famous song, a tune that any Ferengi can sing to this day, was the beautiful ballad, "The Wind in My Ears."

Listen . . . To what's blowing on the wind.
Aaa ooo aaa ooo
A wise man can smell it on the breeze.
Aaa ooo aaa ooo

You can hear it through the rain,
You can hear it on the plain,
And once you hear it,
You'll never be the same.
Yeah yeah yeah.

[nose flute solo]

What is it, that's blowing on the wind?
Aaa ooo aaa ooo
If you stop talking, maybe you'd hear it, too.
Aaa ooo aaa ooo

Profit, that's what I'm saying.
Profit, what the wind is playing.
Profit, that's what I'm earning.
Profit, now your lobes are burning.

So listen . . . to what's blowing on the wind.
Yeah, yeah, yeah.
Stop talking and you can hear it, too.

On a clear, quiet night (and for a modest fee),
a Ferengi can hear the Blessed Exchequer counting
latinum in the Divine Treasury.

Lonz retired from travelling at the ripe old age of one hundred five, after amassing a great fortune and fathering a record number of illegitimate children.

Old Golden Nostril was forever immortalized by the Twenty-Second Rule of Acquisition:

"A wise man can hear profit in the wind."

There's only one kind of businessman more
dangerous than this. . . .

R U L E

#27

t is with a heavy heart that we find ourselves telling the grim tale of Drek, May His Name Live in Infamy. It's hard to believe that the worst villain in Ferengi history started his life as a simple cobbler in the tiny mountain village of Popodoopopop. His reasons remain a mystery, but one thing is certain: Shortly after taking over his father's boot shop, Drek, May His Name Live in Infamy, slashed his prices and began selling footwear at a meager one percent above cost. To add to his sins, Drek M. H. N. L. I. I., created boots of a higher quality than any ever seen on Ferenginar. A single pair of boots made by Drek M. H. N. L. I. I. could last as long as twenty years. Soon, barefoot Ferengi worldwide were travelling to Popodoopopop to get shod.

Other bootmakers were forced to lower their prices and raise their quality to compete with Drek M. H. N. L. I. I. The subsequent run on slither eel hide caused the complete extinction of that most noble of nematodes, the collapse of the hide market, and the utter ruination of thousands of hardworking eel wranglers. And though Drek himself soon died (a shoehorn was found "accidentally" lodged in his throat at the annual bootmakers' convention), the boot market never recovered. The collapse spread to the garment market, then triggered a chain reaction which in a matter of months dragged the entire economy of Ferengi into the worst depression since the Great Monetary Collapse of 9315.

It took almost a hundred fifty years before the economic devastation was finally checked. In the meantime, millions of honest Ferengi found themselves utterly destitute, and all because one madman insisted on selling quality merchandise at a fair price.

So never forget the dire warning of the Twenty-Seventh Rule of Acquisition:

"There's nothing more dangerous than an honest businessman."

RULE
#**31**

A good insult is a thing of beauty, a work of art that endures long after its crafting. Following are ten of the most famous insults in Ferengi history.

1. You couldn't memorize a Rule of Acquisition if it were tattooed to your forehead.
2. You have the business sense of a human. And the body odor of a Klingon.
3. Your house is so tiny you have to leave it to change your mind.
4. Your wife wears clothing.
5. And for five more slips, I'll sell you Ferenginar.
6. When you were born, your father slapped his accountant.
7. You're so stupid, you went into the Bajoran Wormhole looking for tube grubs.
8. Your nose is so tiny, you snort beetle snuff one grain at a time.
9. You're so ugly, you have to wear your headskirt in front of your face.
10. Your lobes are so small you can *oo-mox* with one finger.

If you decide to forgo the classics, please keep in mind the Thirty-First Rule of Acquisition:

> *"Never insult a Ferengi's mother . . . insult*
> *something he cares about instead."*

"Moogie." (Andrea Martin)

Some would call this groveling. To a good businessman,
it's tactical. It also impresses the females. Note the
admiration in Pel's (Hêlen Udy) eyes.

RULE

33

To my beloved Publisher,

It is with much pleasure that I thank you for the latinum delivered to me as an advance on the forthcoming <u>Legends of the Ferengi.</u> In return, I am delighted to deliver this, the commentary on the Thirty-Third Rule of Acquisition. I'd like this opportunity to say, for the record, what an honor it's been to work for you. To say that your treatment of me has been fair and equitable would be a vast understatement. I am in awe of your fairness, your good judgment, and your business acumen. I also think you are as attractive as you are wise. Your lobal cartilage is truly magnificent, and the texture of your nose wrinkles denotes a wealth of olfactory instinct.

Please note that when I said I was being paid less than a starving vole merchant and I wouldn't write this book if you held a phaser to my head, it was just a jocular expression of good fellowship. Subsequent remarks that your royalty statements were steaming stacks of lying worm dung were made while I was recovering from a severe ear infection and under prescribed medication.

And so I end this missive grovelling in the hope that you will find my meager scratching fit for publication and further financial remuneration. May your publishing empire continue to grow and may your latinum shine forever.

Respectfully yours,
Quark, Son of Keldar

Just a reminder from the people who brought you the Thirty-Third Rule of Acquisition:

"It never hurts to suck up to the boss."

R U L E
#**34** and #**35**

Some of the most exciting by-products of the Ferengi-Lytasian Conflict (18101-18105), the only interstellar war ever fought by the Ferengi Alliance, are the numerous and highly collectible souvenir merchandise produced to bolster morale. Some notable examples:

"Lytasians Break Wind" Headskirts. Original Price 1.65 strips of latinum, current value 22.94 strips.

"Marauder Mo, Hero of Ferenginar" Action Figure. Original Price 5 strips of latinum, current value 94.75 strips.

"Marauder Mo, Hero of Ferenginar" Action Figure in original stasis box with "Marauder Mo" Plastic Plasma Whip. Current value 572.5 strips.

"Rally Round the Latinum, Boys" Audio Recording by the Loog Twins. Originally 10 strips of latinum, current value mnt 12,302, nr-mnt 8,992, ex 7025, vg 3021.

"Loose Lips Sink Starships" Poster. Originally distributed free of charge by the Ferengi Morale Office (FerMO), current value vf 1200, f 650.

Oddly enough, the end of the war brought its own series of highly prized collectibles. Among the most sought after items are:

"Hug a Lytasian" Headskirts. Original Price 2.15 strips of latinum, current value 20.5 strips.

"Relief Worker Mo, Rebuilder of Lytasia" Action Figure. Original Price 15 strips of latinum, current value 172.25 strips.

"Relief Worker Mo, Rebuilder of Lytasia" Action Figure in original stasis box with "Relief Worker Mo" Plasma Decoupler and complete set of Self-Sealing Stem Bolts. Current value 2390 strips.

"All We Are Saying . . . Is Give Lytasia a Chance" Audio Recording by the Toob Wyrms. Originally 12.3 strips of latinum,

War or peace—it's all the same to a Ferengi. As long
as there's profit—or at least *oo-mox* with a female
(Mary Kay Adams)—at the end of it.

current value mnt 10,950, nr-mnt 7300, ex 5592, vg 1003.

"Invest in Lytasia, Resort World of the Future" Poster.
Originally distributed free of charge by the Lytasian
Redevelopment Fund (LyReF), current value vf 34, f 12.

The authors of this book currently have all of the above in
stock and will consider any reasonable offer.

All of which only goes to prove the Thirty-Fourth Rule of
Acquisition:

"War is good for business,"

and its corollary, the Thirty-Fifth Rule of Acquisition:

"Peace is good for business."

RULE
#**40**

Ferengi are a busy people. And busy people don't have time to read. Or write. And let's face it, you could fill a black hole with the number of writers who have starved to death through lack of latinum. So there aren't a lot of books on Ferenginar. Oh, every Ferengi household has at least one copy of the Rules of Acquisition. But that's a religious tome and doesn't really count. (Modesty prohibits us from mentioning that with the publication of the *Legends of the Ferengi* there now will be two required texts in every Ferengi home.) As far as Ferengi recreational reading is concerned . . . forget it. In a culture where holosuites are everywhere and literacy is a pricey educational option, books just don't cut it. With one notable exception: The infamous *The Arduous Journey of T'lana on the Road to Enlightenment, or Vulcan Love Slave.* By Anonymous.

Theories abound concerning the true identity of the author of this towering literary achievement. Some credit Grand Nagus Zek, others the Vulcan poetess T'vora, who actually did visit Ferenginar the year before *V.L.S.* was published. But those in the know, and there are more of them than you might think, put their money on Ferenginar's most respected holodrama critic, Iskel the Unimpressed. True, his review of *V.L.S.* was scathing, insulting, and vitriolic, but not long after he called *V.L.S.* a "tawdry, excessively sexual, puerile exercise appealing to the lowest value of the common gutter Ferengi," book sales soared. Get it? Iskel's bad review powered sales of the book as surely as warp engines power starships, and months later Iskel retired, suddenly and inexplicably one of the richest men in the Ferengi Alliance.

For those of you less enlightened than T'lana, we offer up the book's famous final passage:

Shmun placed a tube worm in the corner of his mouth and slowly sucked it up past his full, cruel lips. He stared flat-eyed at T'lana, her nubile Vulcan form backlit by the open window. She inhaled deeply, her breasts rising as her chest filled with the moist, fecund air of Ferenginar. He could see the hunger in her face as she turned to him, her well-shaped pointed ears tensing with desire.

Mixing greed and *oo-mox* is high-risk
behavior. Play it safe.

"You saved my life," she whispered.

"I only accept payment in latinum," Shmun smirked.

*T'lana melted under his arrogant gaze. "I love you," she
said. "Will you accept a bank draft?"*

*Shmun knew then that she was his. Licking away the last
few drops of worm juice from his lips, Shmun strode confident-
ly forward, sweeping her into his arms. "Everything's negotiable,
Bright Eyes," he sneered.*

*T'lana reached down, and with one hand, stroked his burning
left lobe. "My Shmun," she purred. Shmun pressed his body against
hers. As her delicate fingers teased his lobe, he could feel her free
hand crawling like a Romulan fire spider down his body. Her nails
raked his thigh. Shmun stiffened as he felt her hand close warmly
and squeeze tightly around his money pouch. "Nice try," he snick-
ered, and with a mighty heave, he lifted T'lana up into his arms,
took one step forward, and hurled her out the window.*

*T'lana's eyes widened as enlightenment hit her seconds
before she hit the pavement.*

As fine an example of the Fortieth Rule of Acquisition as
we've ever seen.

"She can touch your lobes, but never your latinum."

Nothing typifies the pursuit of profit quite like an
agent (Jeffrey Combs) of the Ferengi
Commerce Authority.

R U L E
#**41**

A long time ago, (longer ago than the parable in Rule One, but not as long ago as the story for Rule #223), on the vast rolling plains of Splort, there lived a Ferengi wooly slug herder named Nix. Now those were the days when being a wooly slug herder really meant something. A simpler, freer time, when Ferengi slugboys rode the plains astride their noble . . . well actually, they weren't astride anything. Wooly slugs are slow-moving and docile creatures who'll do pretty much anything you want if you kick them hard enough. Still, it was a time before Ferengi had met Klingons so they thought slugboys were pretty tough. It was in the days before replicators, before fences, before wooly slug steak was discovered to be a breeding ground for vile and dangerous parasites, when slug herding was big business, and Nix was the biggest slug herder of them all.

And then one day, the plains rumbled like thunder, and a panic came upon the wooly slugs in their millions. For they could sense the coming of their doom, the coming of . . . the dreaded snailosaurus.

Now most people thought that snailosauri had died out some five hundred years ago. Their fossilized shells were used as line camps by the roving slugboys. So the last thing anyone ever expected to see was a live rampaging snailosaurus thundering across the lush plains of Splort. Okay, so maybe rampaging is a bit of poetic license. And maybe thundering is overstating things for the sake of a good yarn. But it was big. And mean. And hungry. And faster than a speeding wooly slug. Maybe not a lot faster. But tell that to a wooly slug. They died by thousands, sucked into the gaping slimy maw of the snailosaurus. And more than a few slugboys went down with them, Ferengi *hors d'oeuvres* complementing the wooly slug feast.

Nix was powerless to do anything except watch his profit margins shrink slowly into the sunset. Desperate, he offered a reward to whomever could slay the ravenous snailosaurus . . . the hand of his first-born daughter in marriage. With an offer like that, Nix kicked back and waited for a stampede of eager, sexually frustrated snailosaurus-hunting slugboys to come knocking at his door. No one showed. And the wooly slug population continued to plummet.

And then one day, from out of the North strode a squinty-eyed, leather-lobed high plains slugboy named . . . well, no one ever did learn his name. They just called him . . . the Slugboy With No Name ("NoName" for short).

NoName was a man with a plan. He told Nix what he needed. A thousand wooly slug hides, seventy seamstresses with seventy high-speed sewing machines, three tons of Grade A slug steak, and several gallons of Eau d'Snail, which at the time was the most popular perfume in all of Ferenginar. The supplies for NoName's plan cost Nix a small fortune, but with his back against the wall, he had no choice but to cooperate. NoName took the seamstresses and all the supplies and locked himself into one of Nix's warehouses. For five days Nix waited for NoName to emerge. On the sixth day, Nix finally lost patience. He entered the warehouse only to find that NoName, the thousand wooly slug hides, the seventy seamstresses, the seventy high-speed sewing machines, the three tons of Grade A slug steak, and the several gallons of Eau d'Snail, not to mention the entire contents of the warehouse, were all gone. All that was left was a gaping hole in the floor and a note.

The note read, "Thanks. I needed this stuff a lot more than you do." Three days later, the snailosaurus choked on the thighbone of an especially burly slugboy. Nix's ranch was saved. But that's not the end of the story. Eight months later, in the city of Binx, half a world away from the plains of Splort, a new clothing designer opened his showroom for business. The soon to be famous "Clothing by ?" began the planet-wide craze for wooly slug sweaters, scented with Eau d'Snail. Buy one, get a Grade A slug steak for free. What Ferengi could pass up a bargain like that?

Suffice it to say the Slugboy with No Name had remembered the Forty-First Rule of Acquisition,

"Profit is its own reward."

R U L E
#**44**

Now when Nix (last seen in Rule Forty-One) got older, he retired from the wooly slug business. It's said he never could sleep soundly again while on the plains of Splort. To him, the nightly keening of the Splort winds sounded like a snailosaurus ceaselessly chomping on poor innocent wooly slugs. So he left the plains and spent the rest of his life indulging in his secret passion, breeding Sleekback Racing Beetles.

Before long Nix owned a stable of the fastest racing beetles on all of Ferenginar. And his pride and joy were two twin . . . what do you call young beetles? Beetlekids? Beetlefillies? Beetlelets? Whatever. They were fast, and they were named "Wisdom" and "Luck." Now Wisdom was an even-tempered beetle, mild, obedient, and true. She responded immediately to the merest urging of her beetlejockey. But her sister Luck was a vicious, evil, disobedient beast. Beetlejockey after beetlejockey was thrown from her sleek shell and trampled by her many legs. But if Wisdom was fast, Luck was faster. When she ran, none could catch her.

Now Nix's still-unmarried daughter, Duwain, loved the racing beetles almost as much as her father. But if she loved the beetles, she loved the beetlejockeys even more. Many a night she would stay up late with the jockeys, drinking fermented wormwine and walking among them indecently clothed. The night before the annual Latinum Mandible, the greatest stakes race of the entire racing beetle circuit, Duwain held one of her notorious parties. The beetlejockeys drank late into the night, and many gallons of wormwine were consumed.

The next morning, the morning of the great race, Koob, Nix's best jockey, awoke bleary-eyed and worm-headed. He went down to the stables to saddle up his mount. Now Koob knew he was scheduled to ride Wisdom, Luck being too mean-spirited and unpredictable to ever be trusted in a high-stakes race. But even on his best days, Koob was not the brightest of jockeys. And this was not one of his best days, not after a long night of

There are all kinds of wisdom, and all kinds of luck.
Know the difference.

wormwine, moonlight, and Duwain. That's right, you guessed it. When Koob rode out of that stable, he had his feet firmly planted in the stirrups of the wrong beetle. He left Wisdom behind and put his fate and his backside on Luck.

On the first lap, Luck took the lead. On the second, she was ahead by two lengths. By the third lap, no one could catch her. But on the fourth lap, Luck turned. No one knows why. Maybe she got bit by a beetlelouse, maybe she got a speck of dust in one of her compound eyes, or maybe she just got tired of being chased by all those other damned beetles. But whatever the reason, Luck spun around on her hind legs and, with Koob holding on for dear life, charged headlong and red-eyed into the pack, colliding with the other beetles at nearly fifty kilometers per hour.

In moments what started out as a pleasant afternoon race was turned into a scene of horrific carnage. Beetles and their riders lay strewn about the track, their many limbs tangled and broken. Duwain rushed down to the field, searching desperately for her fallen lover. She found him, lying mangled and imbedded in the shattered carapace of his steed. And as Duwain cradled Koob's head in her lap, he croaked out his last words . . . "Wrong beetle."

Too late, Koob had learned one of life's essential lessons, the Forty-Fourth Rule of Acquisition,

"Never confuse wisdom with luck."

R U L E
#47

They still talk about him, in the little town of Shnoo. The stranger who came to town on the four-fifteen floater. Eyewitnesses say it looked like a plasma storm was stepping down the boarding ramp. But that was no plasma storm, that was Flus, wearing a suit of live, genetically engineered electric eels. No one had ever seen anything like it. The whole town gathered around him, marveling at his writhing glow. It's said the good-natured Flus stayed up all night drinking with the inhabitants of Shnoo, letting them marvel at his prismatic coat of light. Finally, just before dawn, the bleary-eyed townspeople shuffled off to bed, still muttering in awe at Flus's finery.

They awoke late in the day, only to find their homes looted of every last slip of latinum. Flus was nowhere to be seen. It took months, but the investigators finally realized what had happened. The live eels in Flus's coat had wriggled off his body, slipped into the homes of the sleeping Shnooites, swallowed their hard-earned latinum (everyone knows that latinum is indigestible to eels), and slithered back to their master. Flus merely had to wait for them to excrete the latinum in order to become a fairly wealthy man.

Not long thereafter, a visiting Bolian got off the four-fifteen wearing a suit made entirely of form-fitting energy fields. The Shnooites took one look at his eye-catching outfit and set upon him in a demented frenzy of revenge. The innocent Bolian was beaten severely about the head and torso and spent the next four weeks in the hospital.

The people of Shnoo had learned the hard way that there was great wisdom in the Forty-Seventh Rule of Acquisition:

*"Never trust a man wearing a better suit
than your own."*

They used to say, "Beware Romulans bearing gifts."
Nowadays it's "Beware exiled members of the Obsidian
Order (Andrew Robinson) who offer to hem your trousers."

Doesn't this grin just melt your lobes?

R U L E
#**48**

Every culture is faced with the necessity of teaching its children about the dangers of real life. In most societies, these lessons are taught by telling horror stories featuring some nightmarish figure, the "Bogeyman" of Earth, the Klingons' "Keeper of the Dishonored Dead," or the "Nameless Traitor" of Cardassia. On Ferenginar this figure of supernatural dread is known as the "Smiling Partner."

Ferengi children lose many a good night's sleep cowering in fear at the thought of this terrible creature. Though the stories vary, its *modus operandi* is always the same. The Smiling Partner pretends to be your friend. He offers you a fair and profitable deal. He's generous, likable, and sympathetic to your needs. And of course, he always smiles. But then, the moment after you sign the contract, those smiling teeth turn into razor-sharp blades that crunch down on your lobes and tear them from your head. And as you lie there, blood pouring from the stumps of your ears, the Smiling Partner . . . laughs.

Hahahahahahahahahahahahahahahahahahahahahaha-hahahaha.

It's no wonder that no Ferengi child ever forgets the Forty-Eighth Rule of Acquisition:

"The bigger the smile, the sharper the knife."

RULE

#52

The following posting was made on the Ferengi Commodities Exchange in the Desiccated Collectibles Market.

OFFERED:

THIRTY-FIVE DISKS OF VACUUM DESICCATED FLYNK!!!! Famous holo-performer, dead at fifty. World renowned star of the wildly popular SWAMP KING series found dead in notorious Kefkan accommodation house of beetle snuff overdose. Grand Nagus Zek declares DAY OF MOURNING for actor voted seven years in a row SEXIEST LOBES on Ferenginar. Winner of the GOLDEN LOBE™ for his performance in PRIVATEER OF THE SWAMPWAYS, the first of the SWAMP KING series. Credited with giving the SWAMP KING both his swashbuckling style and his famous catchphrase . . . "Never ask when you can take." Please note: Due to his indulgent lifestyle, there is an extremely LIMIT-ED SUPPLY of Flynk available. Regretfully, much of his mass was too deteriorated to withstand proper desiccation. SO BUY NOW while there's still some Flynk left! And you too can be . . . a SWAMP KING!!!!!

Caution: Due to unusually high levels of wormwine, beetle snuff, tuberessent oil, dex-tramethametroheblezine, and other contaminants present in his remains, Flynk is high-ly combustible. Please keep disks away from open flames.

Flynk may be gone, but his most famous line has been immortalized as the Fifty-Second Rule of Acquisition:

"Never ask when you can take."

There's no moment quite so special as when a Ferengi child
first utters the word, "Mine!"

You could all stand to take a lesson from Morn
(Mark Shepherd).

RULE
57

A TRIBUTE

M . . ."M" is for morning. Each and every morning he stands outside my door, big soulful eyes waiting for me to arrive and open the door to my oasis, so he can slake his mighty thirst. Honor him.

O . . ."O" is for overindulgence. No matter how much he drinks, how much he eats, how much he gambles, it's never enough. His vast appetite knows no bounds. He is secure in the belief that if some is good, more is better. Bless him.

R . . ."R" is for resources. And his are seemingly endless. Where all his latinum comes from, I never ask. After all, it's not my business, is it? All I care about is that he spends it. And spends it at Quark's. Which he does. Cherish him.

N . . ."N" is for nice. In all my years of knowing him, he's never exchanged an unpleasant word with another customer. He's never started a brawl, thrown a beer mug, or missed a payment on his tab. He's a gentle, sweet-tempered man, who wouldn't hurt a fly. True, he did once eat another customer's pet spiderpoodle, but to be fair, the spiderpoodle was left on the bar unattended, and he mistook it for an *hors d'oeuvre*. He was very sorry afterwards and has never eaten a spiderpoodle since. Forgive him.

M . . . O . . . R . . . N. . . . Put them all together, and they spell "MORN." Best customer, truest friend. Love him.

As you can see, I am proud to practice the Fifty-Seventh Rule of Acquisition:

*"Good customers are as rare as latinum
—treasure them."*

RULE
#58

Now, Ferengi may not care much for sculpture, they may not care much for paintings, and they definitely don't care about books . . . but music . . . that's another story. If you don't believe me, check out Rule Twenty-Two. Nothing makes Ferengi lobes vibrate like a good song.

And no one ever vibrated Ferengi lobes like "Success." Four impoverished young Ferengi from Kidneypond, Success became the best-selling recording act in Ferengi history, playing sold-out concerts all over the globe. Amongst their most famous recordings were "I Wanna Hold Your Moneybelt," "Pay, Pay Me Now," and "Luki in a Floater with Latinum." And who can forget their chart-busting ballad "Never Ask When You Can Take" a.k.a. "Ballad of the Swamp King" from the compilation album *A Tribute to Flynk: Twenty-Seven Artists Get Together to Make Money off a Dead Star*?

But perhaps no event better defined the impact of Success than that fateful evening at the Isle of Grub Festival. Billed as "Five Days of Music, *Oo-mox*, and Merchandising," the Isle of Grub Festival was attended by almost a million rabid Success fans, all awaiting the arrival of their idols. But as fate would have it, Grymi Success, the group's popular lead windsqueezer, decided to spend that day sitting wrapped in a tube grub harvesting sack with his new wife, Pino. (Don't ask why. Pino was a Bolian performance artist and liked to do these kinds of things.) Without Grymi to lead them, Success had no choice but to back out of the concert, and left immediately for a vacation on Risa.

So, when on the fifth night, after over a hundred hours of frenzied anticipation, the mecho-accordian band "Sound of One Lobe Flapping" took the stage instead of Success, close to a million furious fans forgot all about Music, *Oo-mox*, and Merchandising and stormed the stage in a frenzy of destruction. Every structure on the Isle of Grub was burned to the ground, over a hundred thousand rioting Success fans were injured, and all seven members of Sound of One Lobe Flapping disappeared without a trace.

Make no mistake; if there's profit involved, a Ferengi
can party with the best of them.

Shortly afterwards, Success put out an album entitled *In
Memory of the Fallen, a Tribute to the Tragedy at Grub*, featuring
the hit single "Grymi Says He's Sorry." It sold a hundred million
copies.

Which just goes to prove the Fifty-Eighth Rule of Acquisition:

"There is no substitute for success."

R U L E
#59

ow, I'd like to take this opportunity to answer a few of the letters I received after the publication of my runaway best-seller (still available in bookstores) *The Ferengi Rules of Acquisition*. Here's a typical example:

Dear Quark,
You are such a wise man. I was hoping you could give me some advice. I've inherited several thousand bars of latinum and don't know what to do with it. Can you help me?
Signed,
Pockets Full of Latinum

Dear Pockets,
My advice to you is simple. Hire me as your investment broker. For a tiny fraction of your profits (not to exceed fifty percent) I will manage your entire portfolio. I do this because I am a kind man, and you are very, very . . . deserving of my help. I guarantee by the time I'm done, you will never have to worry about your latinum again.
Yours in profit,
Quark

Dear Quark,
I am dating a beautiful and insatiable Betazoid woman. No matter what I do, and I do a lot, it never seems to be enough. I love her very much, but I don't seem able to satisfy her. You showed so much wisdom in your best-selling book The Ferengi Rules of Acquisition *(still available in bookstores), that I am confident you will be able to advise me in this matter. What should I do?*
Signed,
Unlucky in Love

Hew-mons say talk is cheap. If only they knew . . .

Dear Unlucky,

I feel your pain. Enclosed please find a prepaid ticket to Deep Space Nine. As soon as you receive it, give it to your girlfriend and send her to me. Don't wait. Do it now!

Okay. Is she gone? Good. I await her. I promise you, she will not leave this station without achieving a state of complete and utter satisfaction. No matter how long it takes, no matter how much experimentation is required, I will find a way to end her suffering, and yours as well. Rest assured, she'll be in good hands.

Your humble servant,
Quark

Keep those cards and letters coming. What better way for me to illustrate the Fifty-Ninth Rule of Acquisition:

"Free advice is seldom cheap."

R U L E
#60

Sometimes people ask me, "Quark, why are the Rules of Acquisition so important to memorize?" I usually just say, "That's a pretty stupid question." But for you dense hew-mons, perhaps I should just give you an example of what can happen when you forget to follow an important Rule.

MEMO TO CAPTAIN SISKO
FROM QUARK, PROPRIETOR QUARK'S ENTERPRISES, INC.
In regards to your question of why power consumption at Quark's Bar (a wholly owned subsidiary of Q.E.I.) has increased dramatically during this last month, the answer is quite simple: increased Klingon usage of the holosuites. As you may be aware, full-impact Klingon Exercise Holoprograms drain much more energy than my usual, more soothing fare. Additionally, Klingons tend to have considerably more endurance than my other clients, so average holosuite booking times have also increased. In the interests of continued good relations with the Klingons, I ask that my power allocation be raised accordingly.

MEMO TO CAPTAIN SISKO
FROM ROM, DIAGNOSTIC AND REPAIR TECHNICIAN, JUNIOR GRADE
You wanted to know why my brother's bar is using more power. The answer is simple. . . replicator inefficiency. His replicators are very old, and since I have begun work in the Engineering Department, I have not had time to conduct proper maintenance on his system. As a result, his replicator power:output ratio has increased from 2.35418:1 to a new high of 4.17455:1. As soon as my workload eases up (in approximately seven to eight months) I will address this problem. Until then, I ask that Quark's power allocation be raised accordingly.

When dealing with a hew-mon (Avery Brooks),
always get your story straight.

MEMO TO QUARK
FROM CAPTAIN BENJAMIN LAFAYETTE SISKO (YOUR LANDLORD)

PLEASE BE ADVISED THAT AFTER REVIEWING YOUR MEMO AND THAT OF YOUR BROTH-
ER ROM, I AM OFFICIALLY REDUCING YOUR MONTHLY POWER ALLOCATION. BEFORE YOU
COMPLAIN THAT THIS IS UNFAIR, YOU SHOULD KNOW THAT I'M WELL AWARE OF THE
LIVE VOLE FIGHTS THAT YOU HAVE BEEN CONDUCTING AFTER HOURS IN YOUR BAR (IN
CLEAR VIOLATION OF YOUR LEASE). I SUSPECT THAT ENDING THE VOLE FIGHTS SHOULD
REDUCE YOUR POWER CONSUMPTION BACK TO YOUR NORMAL LEVELS. ON THE OTHER
HAND, IF THE BAR CONTINUES TO CONSUME ENERGY AT ITS CURRENT RATE, YOU CAN
PONDER THE ERRORS OF YOUR WAYS FROM INSIDE YOUR USUAL HOLDING CELL. HAVE
A NICE DAY.

See what I mean?

So when you start committing the Rules to memory, perhaps you
should begin with the Sixtieth Rule of Acquisition:

"Keep your lies consistent."

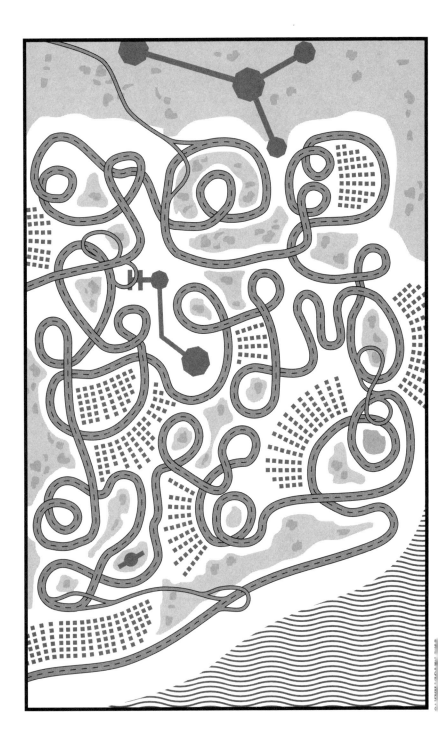

R U L E
#62

As we all know, the leading cause of death on Ferenginar remains accidental vehicular collision. This has been true for hundreds of years (barring the snail steak food-poisoning epidemic of 11,902) and will doubtless be true for hundreds more. People often ask, are Ferengi really that inept when it comes to vehicular navigation? I mean, how hard is it to control a skimmer? Frankly, it's pretty easy. Yet the skimmer death toll continues to mount. And I can sum up the problem in one word: Ferengi Road Design. (Okay, that's three words, but it's one thought.)

On the left is an aerial view of the most heavily traveled skimmerway on Ferenginar, Skimmer Interchange 405 just outside West Wormwood.

As you can see, the pattern of this interchange clearly forms the ideograms "Drink Slug-o-Cola! It's Good For You!" Subliminal Marketeers for the Yand Corporation determined centuries ago that frequently travelled skimmer routes become imprinted on the driver's brain. So what better way to increase product awareness than to make the very roads themselves advertising logos? Slug-o-Cola, who pioneered this technique, used it to completely take over the soft drink market from Eelwasser, their closest competitor.

Unfortunately, the tricky turn required to complete the ideogram for "Slug" has proven almost impossible to navigate on a rainy day. And it rains almost every day on Ferenginar.

Still, subsidies from Slug-o-Cola have made the Ferengi Skimmerway Construction Department one of the most well-endowed public trusts on all of Ferenginar. And it's hard to argue with success.

So drink Slug-o-Cola!

Just watch out for that last turn.

And remember the Sixty-Second Rule of Acquisition:

"The riskier the road, the greater the profit."

R U L E
65

I t's not giving away any government secrets to say that when it comes to the art of warfare, Ferengi have never advanced much beyond stick figures. Though Ferengi love to crush their opponents across the negotiating table, the thought of disemboweling someone, or even worse, being disemboweled, leaves the valiant sons of Ferenginar feeling a little queasy. So it's no surprise that the Ferengi armed forces, which rely entirely on volunteers, have always had trouble keeping their ranks at full strength.

In fact, it was nearly impossible to get a young Ferengi male to put on a uniform until the Hupyrian conflict. Now, the Hupyrian conflict was one of those nasty little wars where it's difficult to tell friend from foe, soldier from civilian. But Grand Nagus Oblat had vast holdings in on the Hupyrian homeworld, so when the Hupyrian People's Unity Front tried to "liberate" the Nagus's duridium mines, Oblat knew he could no longer stand by and let the senseless conflict impact his stock portfolio. He founded the Ferengi/Hupyrian Friendship Brigade (the famous FHFB) to bring peace to that troubled world. But the fact that Hupyrians are twice as big as Ferengi, and had perfected the art of guerilla warfare during centuries of pointless bloodsoaked conflicts, dulled the enthusiasm of potential recruits.

That is, until word leaked back to Ferenginar of a delightful new stimulant discovered by the few brave (and extremely well paid) FHFB recruits slogging through the jungles of Northern Hupyria. It seems that when dried, crushed, and inhaled, the common Hupyrian wood beetle generated a sense of well-being and contentment that Ferengi found nearly irresistible.

Before long, packets of Hupyrian beetle snuff began appearing all over Ferenginar, at prices far higher than the average Ferengi could afford. Though the demand for the intoxicating and highly addictive beetle snuff rose steadily, the supply, at least on Ferenginar, remained tight. Oblat, who after all was a Nagus and thus nobody's fool, quickly announced that from here on out all Ferengi military personnel would be supplied with one free can-

Beware the world leader who says he doesn't inhale.

ister of beetle snuff per week. Enlistment soared. Hupyrian casualties mounted, and within a year the Nagus's duridium mines were as safe as if they were located in the shadow of the Tower of Commerce itself.

And to this day, Ferengi military recruitment posters still bear the battle cry of the FHFB, which has been immortalized as the Sixty-Fifth Rule of Acquisition:

"Win or lose, there's always Hupyrian beetle snuff."

R U L E
#**75**

erengi don't usually discuss this with outsiders, but even now, in the great age of space travel, Ferengi don't really like to leave home. For one thing, it's hard to get good tube grubs off-world. And even though the weather on Ferenginar may leave something to be desired, it is consistent. Besides, when you get right down to it, most known cultures insist that their females be clothed and allowed to speak.

In fact, for centuries it was nearly impossible to get Ferengi to leave their silent, naked wives, and wriggling, well-stocked larders and head into space. This resulted in the great Overpopulation Crisis of 17231, when it was said that no raindrops ever hit the ground because there were so damn many Ferengi heads in the way.

Then one day, a rumor spread that a Ferengi prospector named Mad Zook had found massive deposits of latinum on the distant world of Chimera Pi. Soon Ferengi homes everywhere bore the sign "Gone to Chimera." And it wasn't long thereafter that rumors of other mother lodes on even more distant planets drifted back to Ferenginar.

Eventually the rumors were traced back to the Ferengi Office of Population Control, but by then, it was too late. Billions of Ferengi had sought their fortunes in space. And when they got there, they discovered an interesting thing. Aliens. Or, in the Ferengi parlance . . . *Gooblatrupyobs*, which literally translates into "Bank accounts without brains." Now, on Ferenginar, the only people you can try to exploit are other Ferengi. And they're a suspicious, thrifty, economically savvy bunch, who are just as likely to be the exploiters as the exploited. Too often, negotiations between Ferengi end up in stalemates. But *Gooblatrupyobs* . . . that's another story.

So maybe Mad Zook was a figment of the government's imagination, and maybe there is no Chimera Pi, but as long as there's a *Gooblatrupyob* born every 0.000021 seconds, then Ferengi will travel to the stars.

The meek can inherit the Earth. The Ferengi
will take the rest.

Thus there's more than a grain of truth to the Seventy-Fifth
Rule of Acquisition:

> *"Home is where the heart is . . . but the*
> *stars are made of latinum."*

The important thing is to always keep your opponent (Rene Auberjonois) guessing.

RULE
#**76**

I t's said that humor doesn't translate. What makes one species smile makes another grimace. Take, for instance, the "comedy" entertainments produced on Earth. With the exception of the comic genius of "The Three Stooges" (and even then, only those shorts featuring Shemp), Ferengi find humans humorless, dour, sanctimonious boobs who are more fun to laugh at than laugh with. So when I describe Ferengi humor, I will understand if other species scratch their collective heads.

Let's take for example the two greatest comedians of Ferenginar during the Golden Age of Silly Bwah-hah-hahs (see, already I can tell you're not getting this): Gormie Gormatop, famous for his comic character "Klang the Incontinent Klingon," and Dirf, Son of Dorf, who left them rolling in the aisles with his on-the-mark portrayal of "Shlork the Stuttering Vulcan." To this day every Ferengi instantly recognizes their famous tag lines, "I will kill you where you stand! But first I must visit waste extraction!" and, "It's n-n-n-n-n-not log-g-gical." I'm telling you, these guys were funny!

They also hated one another. In fact the Gormie/Dirf feud (or, as Dirf would prefer, the Dirf/Gormie feud) is one of the defining characteristics of the Golden Age of Silly Bwah-hah-hahs. Not only would these two not share the same bill, they wouldn't even perform in the same cities. If Gormie played East Morvin, Dirf would never set foot in the place again. And if Dirf headlined in Tregas, Gormie wouldn't even say the word "Tregas" as long as he lived. Back in the Golden Age of Silly Bwah-hah-hahs (I can tell the term is starting to grow on you), you were either a Dirf city or a Gormie city.

And then one day, the impossible happened. It was announced that Gormie and Dirf would be appearing together on the same program, a gala memorial service commemorating the thirtieth anniversary of the death of the Swamp King himself . . . Flynk. It turned out that both Dirf and Gormie were rabid Flynk fans.

You see, Flynk gave Gormic his first break, playing a cabin boy in one of Flynk's last films, *Swamp King at Sunset*. And everyone knows Dirf was married (briefly) to Flynk's eighth wife. So Gormie extended the hand of friendship to his old foe, Dirf, and suggested they appear together for the sake of Flynk (and the potential of the biggest box-office gross in Memorial Service history). Gormie even went so far as to promise Dirf that he could be the closing act. To the surprise of everyone, including probably Gormie, Dirf accepted.

It's said that more Ferengi paid to see the live transmission of the Flynk tribute than paid for any other event in Ferengi history. And though the Swamp King remained a popular figure even in death, everyone knew they were tuning in to see Dirf and Gormie share a stage for the first time.

So imagine the shock that reverberated across Ferenginar when Gormie stepped out on stage dressed as Dirf's beloved "Shlork the Stuttering Vulcan." As Dirf looked on in horror, Gormie proceeded to do Dirf's entire act. Gormie had planned this moment for years, secretly studying recordings of Dirf and waiting for his moment to strike. As the audience convulsed in laughter, Gormie stripped off his Shlork suit, to reveal his Klang costume, and proceeded to run through a brilliant rendition of the Incontinent Klingon, causing people all over Ferenginar to soil their own undergarments from hysterical laughter. After concluding his act with the brilliant line "I would kill you where you stand, but it's n-n-n-n-n-not log-g-g-gical!" Gormie stepped off the stage just in time to see Dirf being taken away by Emergency Medical Services (Incorporated). Gormie later admitted that he never even liked Flynk. Dirf never performed in public again.

Gormie had gotten the last laugh by remembering the Seventy-Sixth Rule of Acquisition:

"Every once in a while, declare peace . . . it confuses the hell out of your enemies."

RULE
#79

F.C.A. Liquidation of the Assets of Doctor Solev of Vulcan (resident of Ferenginar 18211–18217)

Items to be liquidated:

1. One (1) Ancient Ferengi Castle, located in the scenic Gothis Mountains. Seven bedrooms, extensive dungeons, towers, battlements. Top floor of keep converted into modern science and medical facility. A rustic fixer-upper.

2. One (1) Genetic Reconfiguring Matrix.

3. One (1) Stasis Chamber, Vulcan manufacture, some burn marks.

4. One (1) Lightning Harnesser, affixed to castle tower with lightning rod attached, seventeen meters long.

5. One (1) Bio-bed (eight feet long), extensive stains. Could make a great coffee table/conversation piece.

6. Seven (7) Severed Ferengi Hands (four left, three right).

7. Thirteen (13) Severed Ferengi Feet, some with legs attached.

8. Forty-two (42) Pair Ferengi Lobes, some slightly decomposed.

9. Three hundred kilos (300k) Assorted Additional Misc. Ferengi Body Parts. Chests, torsos, knees, buttocks, etc.

(Please note: Items 6 through 9 are all stored in individual jars of bio-static liquid. All are used, undesiccated, original owners unknown.)

10. One (1) Diary padd belonging to the deceased. Including notes for a scientific paper, "The Illogic of Death, or, Bringing the Dead to Life, a Noble Experiment."

11. One (1) Scrawled Note, in Vulcan, addressed by the deceased to Professor J. Whales of the Daystrom Institute, consisting of two words . . . "It's alive!" A real collector's item.

12. Seventeen Hundred Twelve (1712) copies of various medical textbooks and journals, all in Vulcan. Many with extensive burn damage. Translate them yourself for fun and profit!

Caution: If a Vulcan (Bertilla Damas) eyes your lobes in this fashion, she may want more than *oo-mox*.

13. One (1) Vulcan Harp, charmingly dented.

14. One (1) Seven Foot, Ten Inch (7'10") Tall Ferenginoid Life form. Semi-sentient. Composed of Ferengi body parts. Very strong. Capable of following simple commands. Will work for electricity. Warning: Do not attempt to feed by hand.

All proceeds from the sale of these items to benefit the estate of Rogi the Pigeon-Toed, Ferengi citizen, graduate of the Laboratory Assistants' Institute of Ferenginar, tragically cut down in the prime of life while under the employ of Doctor Solev (see warning on item 14).

Perhaps Rogi would be alive today if only he'd followed the Seventy-Ninth Rule of Acquisition:

"Beware of the Vulcan greed for knowledge."

RULE

#**82**

A perfect summation of the Eighty-Second Rule of Acquisition:

"The flimsier the product, the higher the price."

RULE

#85

Dear Krax,

It has come to my attention that you are in negotiations to write a book entitled <u>Origins and Examples of the Ferengi Rules of Acquisition</u>. If I understand this correctly, you intend to relate brief parables which will illustrate and explain the origins and underlying philosophies of the Rules of Acquisition. Personally, I find such an undertaking morally repugnant. That you, the son of Grand Nagus Zek, may his latinum always shine, would consent to such a project makes me ill.

Have you no common decency? Would all the latinum in the galaxy be worth such a vile betrayal of your people and principles? Need I remind you that the Rules of Acquisition are the most sacred precepts of our culture? Simply quoting them to outsiders (as Quark, son of Keldar, did in his best-selling book, <u>The Ferengi Rules of Acquisition</u>) is one thing. But explaining them in detail, laying their wisdom bare for inferior species to profit from? My heart freezes when I consider the implications of such an action.

I urge you, as a fellow Ferengi, to cease and desist from this destructive and ignoble course of action immediately. If not, I believe you will go down in history as the catalyst that destroyed the Ferengi Alliance. And I pity you when the Blessed Exchequer balances your books.

Respectfully yours,

A concerned and loyal citizen of Ferenginar

Bcc to: My Beloved Publisher, Earth.

Hopefully that'll put an end to any plans Krax has to horn in on our market. The little creep will probably be too racked with fear and guilt to write his own name, let alone a book.

Your loyal employee,

Quark

enc.

You can almost smell the wood burning.

A nice illustration, if I do say so myself, of the Eighty-Fifth Rule of Acquisition:

"Never let the competition know what you're thinking."

73

Some Rules make good bedtime tales. Then there are those
that will put you into a coma . . .

RULE
#89, #202,
#218

Now we come to one of the darker, or at least duller, chapters in Ferengi history: the time of Grand Nagus Smeet, also known as Smeet the Obvious (r. 11903–11912). His reign amounted to nothing less than nine years of sheer, unadulterated boredom.

So why am I even bothering to bring this up? Why hit such a sour note in what is essentially a frolicking tale of a happy-go-lucky culture? Simple. As hard as it is to believe, the fact remains that Smeet wrote no less than three Rules of Acquisition. So I present them to you now. You be the judge. Was this guy boring? Or was he BORING?

(Listen to me. I've become boring just talking about him.)

Here they are. Smeet's Rules: The Eighty-Ninth Rule of Acquisition:

"Ask not what your profits can do for you, but what you can do for your profits."

The Two Hundred Second Rule of Acquisition:

"The justification for profit is profit."

And the Two Hundred Eighteenth Rule of Acquisition:

"Always know what you're buying."

You can wake up now!

Ira Steven Behr and Robert Hewitt Wolfe

RULE
#94

The following is the oldest known piece of writing in the Ferengi language. It was found carved on a cave wall in the Caverns of Sogg.

Scholars have debated for millennia about the meaning of this crude etching by an unknown author. Only three primitive heiroglyphics are used in the statement. The symbol for female, the symbol for profit, and the symbol for male repeated fourteen times (if you haven't bothered counting them yourself). It can never be known what the author's intent was when he took his chisel to that virgin piece of stone, but one thing is eminently clear.

The female has the money and the men are dead.

Which in this author's opinion demonstrates that from the dawn of time, Ferengi males have been aware of the principles behind the Ninety-Fourth Rule of Acquisition:

"Females and finances don't mix."

R U L E
#95

While it's true that most of the wisdom found in the Rules of Acquisition originated in the minds of brilliant Ferengi, on rare occasion outsiders have proven to have the right stuff when it comes to profit.

Take the Breen. Other races know little about this elusive and chilly people. Even we Ferengi do not claim to be experts on Breen psychology, philosophy, or mating rituals. All we know is that they like their tube grubs on ice, their icoberry juice frozen solid, and their holosuite fantasies snowy. Still, if we never learn a single other fact about the Breen, they'll always be okay by us. After all, they're the guys who sold us warp drive.

Or to be more specific, one particular guy sold us warp drive. We called him "the Masked Breen" because he never took off the helmet of his spacesuit (of course, neither do the rest of them, but we didn't know that at the time). The Masked Breen appeared on Ferenginar one cold winter day. He was peddling warp-drive technology, and he wasn't going to take "no" for an answer. He was on our world for only two short days, but in that time, he changed our society forevermore. Not only that, he bought our North Pole, our South Pole, seven frozen moons on the outskirts of our solar system, and a half-dozen comets. Now some of you might say that's a lot to pay for warp drive. But what do we need our arctic wastelands for? They're cold. It's bad enough that it rains all the time on Ferenginar. Who needs ice?

The next day, the Masked Breen disappeared, taking with him his moons and comets. The poles are still there. We think.

We'll never forget the Masked Breen, or the powerful and catchy sales pitch he made. Short and to the point, his laconic, vaguely threatening motto was worthy of a Grand Nagus. Therefore it is only fitting that we immortalized it as a Rule of Acquisition. The only one ever written by a non-Ferengi.

So ponder the words of one brilliant Breen, the Ninety-Fifth Rule of Acquisition:

"Expand . . . or die."

Sends cold shivers down your spine, doesn't it?

To coin a phrase: "Engage!"

Dead or alive, real or imaginary—you gotta admit, if you're a Nagus (Max Grodénchik), you're laughing all the way to the Divine Treasury.

RULE
#97

This is the only Rule ever coined by Grand Nagus Untz, also known as Untz the Invisible. Supposedly, Untz dedicated his whole life to profit, focusing on it to such an extent that everything else in his life dropped away. As the story goes, Untz never ate, never drank, never slept, spoke to no one, and saw no one. According to legend, he spent every hour of his life covertly manipulating and controlling the Ferengi economy. How he achieved this remains a bit of a puzzle. After all, by the time he died, it was said that no one had spoken to him in over seventy years.

In fact, there are some Ferengi scholars who claim that Untz never existed. They believe that for his entire reign, Ferenginar had no Grand Nagus at all. And that this Rule is a part of an elaborate cover-up designed to make people believe in Untz.

Still other Ferengi believe Untz never died and is still controlling the Ferengi economy to this day. The No-Untzers and the Eternal-Untzers are so violently opposed to one another that any written statement siding with one or the other invites immediate and deadly reprisal.

Leaving the question, "To Untz or not to Untz?" You decide.

So valid or not, we present to you what is sometimes considered the Ninety-Seventh Rule of Acquisition:

"Enough . . . is never enough."

RULE
#99

"TRUST"

BY QUARKIE, SON OF KELDAR

SECOND YEAR STUDENT, HOPAWUP ACADEMY FOR YOUNG LOBELINGS

ONCE I LOANED MY BROTHER ROM MY MARAUDER MO ACTION FIGURE. HE LOST THE PLASMA WHIP. NOW MY MARAUDER MO HAS NO WHIP. IF THE KLINGONS ATTACK, HE WILL BE DEFENSELESS. NOT ONLY THAT, BUT THE RESALE VALUE OF MY ACTION FIGURE HAS BEEN SEVERELY COMPROMISED.

I TRUSTED ROM.

ONCE I TOLD MY FATHER WHERE I KEPT MY BIRTHDAY LATINUM. NOW IT'S GONE. HE TOOK IT.

I TRUSTED MY FAFA.

ONCE, WHEN I WAS A FIRST YEAR STUDENT AT HOPAWUP ACADEMY, I AGREED TO DO THE ECONOMIC THEORY HOMEWORK OF BLORK, SON OF BLOUT. BUT I DID NOT INSIST ON PAYMENT IN ADVANCE. I STILL HAVE NOT RECEIVED MY FEE.

CHRIS ELIOPOULOS

EVEN THOUGH I HAVE SENT BLORK REGULAR BILLS AND HE IS ACCRUING INTEREST AT AN ALARMING RATE. I MAY HAVE NO RECOURSE BUT TO HIRE A COLLECTIONS AGENT.

I TRUSTED BLORK.

ONCE I SHOWED MY FRIEND GOEM HOW TO OO-MOX HIMSELF. HE TOLD MY MOOGIE ON ME. SHE WAS ANGRY. SHE PUT NUMBING OINTMENT ON MY EARS FOR A MONTH. I DIDN'T HAVE ANY FUN THAT MONTH.

I TRUSTED GOEM.

ONCE YOU ASKED ME TO STAY AFTER SCHOOL AND POLISH THE DESK MONITORS. YOU LEFT ME ALONE IN THE CLASSROOM. YOU THOUGHT YOUR THINGS WERE SAFE INSIDE YOUR LOCKED DESK. BUT THEY WEREN'T. I AM A VERY GOOD LOCKPICK. INSIDE, I FOUND SOME VERY DISTURBING PICTURES OF YOU. YOU WERE AT A FROCK ROOM TALKING WITH FULLY CLOTHED WOMEN. YOU WERE EVEN LETTING THEM TALK TO YOU. YOU ARE A VERY SICK FERENGI AND A DANGER TO SOCIETY. BUT I AM YOUNG AND IMMATURE ENOUGH TO OVERLOOK THAT, AS LONG AS YOU PAY ME THREE SLIPS OF LATINUM PER MONTH FOR THE DURATION OF MY STAY AT HOPAWUP.

YOU TRUSTED ME.

TRUST IS BAD.

CHRIS ELIOPOULOS

As you can see, even as a young lobeling, I understood the Ninety-Ninth Rule of Acquisition:

"Trust is the biggest liability of all."

RULE

#102

Life span of a Misian bogfly: **12 hours**
Life span of a tube grub: **10 weeks**
Shelf life of a chilled tube grub: **7 months**
Time it takes snail juice to spoil: **193 days**
Life span of a wooly slug: **12 years**
Life span of a wooly slug before the extinction of snailosauri:
     not very long
Life span of a snailosaurus: **Don't know. They're all dead.**
Life span of a Grumpackian tortoise (The longest lived organic
life-form in the galaxy): **12,000 years**
Amount of time it would take a Grumpackian tortoise to circle
the DS9 Promenade: **15,000 years**
Life span of a Federation hew-mon: **Approximately 130 years
     but seems a lot longer because it's so boring.**
Life span of a Federation hew-mon working for Starfleet
security (who for some reason are called red-shirts even
though they wear yellow): **Rarely survive beyond the second-
     act break.**
Life span of a Klingon warrior: **Who cares? Any day is a good
     day for one of those smelly psychopaths to die.**
Life span of a Ferengi: **Up to 300 years with proper lobe
     maintenance.**
Shelf life of a bar of latinum: **Forever**
Shelf life of a strip of latinum: **Forever**
Shelf life of a slip of latinum: **Forever**

Do the math yourself, but anyway you figure it, the results
will still validate the Hundred Second Rule of Acquisition:

"Nature decays, but latinum is forever."

Among Ferengi, it's reassuring to know that your
assets will outlive you.

Ira Steven Behr and Robert Hewitt Wolfe

R U L E
#**104**

Since the Rules of Acquisition were written out of order (as I explained in the introduction to my best-selling collector's item *The Ferengi Rules of Acquisition*), the label "One Hundred Four" is quite misleading. This Rule was actually the second Rule ever created. (This may be confusing for those of you who haven't read my other book. Too bad. Go buy it. Or remain confused. It's up to you.)

In the year 207, Grand Nagus Gint, the first Grand Nagus, the Enlightened Prophet of Greed, died in an unfortunate tooth-sharpening accident. Ferengi worldwide went into a deep, dark depression. Gint had not named a successor. Would he turn out to be the first and only Grand Nagus? All of Ferenginar held its breath to find out.

And then, one day, a voice cried out above the wailing and the weeping. "Fear not," it said. "Gint will return to us . . . his mind as sharp as his teeth." The voice belonged to Yost, a charismatic young Ferengi. Yost insisted that if every single Ferengi purchased a Gint memorial figurine and prayed to it nightly, the Blessed Exchequer would release Gint from the Divine Treasury and allow him to descend back down to Ferenginar.

Yost's message swept the planet. It is believed that there were approximately three billion Ferengi alive at that time. But archaeologists have uncovered over eight billion Gint figurines. They're the most common artifact on Ferenginar and are often used to this day as backscratchers (the figurines commonly portray Gint with his arms extended in a gesture of grasping benediction).

But despite this show of pious consumerism, Gint never came back. On the other hand, Yost, who owned a sizable share in the factories manufacturing the figurines, quickly became the richest man on Ferenginar. So rich, in fact, that he himself became the second Grand Nagus. His first official act was to reveal the Hundred and Fourth Rule of Acquisition (or the second Rule, depending on how you count them). And as people

86

On Ferenginar, religion and marketing
go hand in hand.

came to appreciate the truth of this rule, they realized that in some strange way, Yost had truly embodied the spirit of Gint and was a worthy Grand Nagus indeed.

So in honor of Yost, Gint, and eight billion backscratchers, I present to you the Hundred and Fourth Rule of Acquisition:

"Faith moves mountains . . . of inventory."

The universe may abhor a vacuum, but Ferengi abhor
an empty bank account.

RULE
#106

Okay, now let's play a little game. Take the word "poverty," and use its letters to make as many other words as you can. To help you out, I've given you a few examples.

POVERTY
    yet
    over
    toe

Now you try. When you're done, check page 90 for the answers.

_____ _____ _____

_____ _____ _____

_____ _____ _____

_____ _____ _____

_____ _____ _____

_____ _____ _____

_____ _____ _____

_____ _____ _____

_____ _____ _____

_____ _____ _____

_____ _____ _____

_____ _____ _____

_____ _____ _____

_____ _____ _____

ANSWER KEY FOR RULE 106:

P O V E R T Y

over	overt	per	pert
pet	pore	port	pot
prey	prove	pry	rope
ropey	rot	rote	rove
rye	toe	top	tor
tore	toy	trove	try
very	vet	vote	voter
yet	yore		

Now, study this list and consider the wisdom of the One Hundred Sixth Rule of Acquisition:

"There is no honor in poverty."

RULE
#**109**

nlike Klingons, or even hew-mons, Ferengi aren't a bunch of bloodthirsty barbarians who jump at any chance to start a fight. We'd much rather settle our differences with a heated negotiation than a photon torpedo. But sometimes, people try to take advantage of our good nature. Sometimes, they push us too far.

Take the Lytasians, for example. Now lots of theories have been advanced about what started the Ferengi/Lytasian Conflict. But we Ferengi know the truth. It all started with the worst first contact in history. Or to be more precise, it all started with the Sack Incident.

The first meeting between the Ferengi and the Lytasians took place on the Plateau of Drul, on the Lytasian Homeworld. A delegation of distinguished Ferengi, led by Grand Nagus Zek, met a delegation of Lytasians to extend the hand of friendship and offer them membership in the Ferengi Alliance. As usual, we presented them with the traditional, and very generous, gift of a diamond-encrusted latinum bust of Zek himself. The Lytasians appeared properly impressed and gratified. But when the moment came for them to present their own gift, they revealed the vile core of their nature. They handed Grand Nagus Zek, the most revered man in the Ferengi Alliance, a sack. And inside that sack . . . was nothing.

The Lytasians claimed their gift was intended as a great compliment. That by handing Zek that empty bag, they were acknowledging that there was nothing they had that he could possibly want. That to give him anything else would insult his dignity.

But Grand Nagus Zek saw through their squeaky-voiced excuses. With utter contempt, he rose to his feet and uttered those nine famous words that totally humiliated the Lytasians and plunged Ferenginar into a grinding, bloody five-year-long interstellar war.

On the subject of dignity, there's no disputing the
wisdom of Grand Nagus Zek.

And so I offer you here those nine little words that launched
ten thousand ships, immortalized as the One Hundred Ninth
Rule of Acquisition:

"Dignity and an empty sack . . . is worth the sack."

R U L E

III

I t's important to keep in mind that the Rules of Acquisition are more than just dry aphorisms gathered in a book. (Though there's nothing wrong with that. See *The Ferengi Rules of Acquisition* by Quark as told to Ira Steven Behr.) They're rich treasure troves of practical advice, which, if followed closely, are sure to improve every aspect of your life. If you don't believe that, here's an example of how the Rules work for me:

Dear _____ (insert name here),

It's that time of year again. The Bajoran Gratitude Festival is only a few days away. And in keeping with our tradition here at Quark's, we will celebrate the Festival by allowing you, _____ (insert name here), to express your Gratitude to me and to Quark's. I like to think that Quark's isn't just my bar . . . it's your bar, too. And right now, your bar needs a new coat of paint.

Now I know painting isn't always fun. And even a bar like Quark's can be painted in seconds using automated color sprayers. But automated color sprayers are expensive. And besides, think of the satisfaction, the sense of purpose, not to mention the exercise you and customers like you will get by doing the job by hand. And even more than that, think of how it will help ease the burden of guilt that has been weighing so heavily on your shoulders these last few _____ (fill in appropriate amount of time). I know how miserable you must be knowing that your overdue bar tab, which currently stands at _____ (fill in amount due), is placing an unnecessary financial burden on me, and on Quark's.

True, I suppose I could get a couple of Nausicaans to see to the collection of your tab. But the only people who would really enjoy that would be the Nausicaans. And personally if there's one thing I can't abide, it's a cheery Nausicaan.

Now, painting Quark's won't forgive your debt. Hell, it won't

On Ferenginar, there's no such thing as brotherly
love. Binding financial obligations are another
thing entirely.

even reduce it. But it will make you feel better. A lot better than
if you were visited by a Nausicaan. And there's nothing I like so
much as making my customers feel better.

Peldor joi,

Quark, Son of Keldar

Proprietor, Quark's Bar, Grill, Gaming House, and Holosuite
Arcade, a wholly owned subsidiary of Quark Enterprises, Inc.

Dear Rom,

I'm painting the bar tomorrow. Or to be more precise, you and a bunch of deadbeats are painting the bar tomorrow. Be there.

Your loving brother,

Quark, Son of Keldar

Proprietor, Quark's Bar, Grill, Gaming House, and Holosuite Arcade, a wholly owned subsidiary of Quark Enterprises, Inc.

Trust me, by the time they were done, the bar never looked better.

And what do I have to thank for that? The One Hundred Eleventh Rule of Acquisition:

> *"Treat people in your debt like*
> *family . . . exploit them."*

R U L E

#112

et's face it. . . . We've all thought about breaking this Rule at one time or another. I mean, almost every boss has one. Usually the family is rich, so there's the inheritance factor to consider. Plus forbidden fruit is always the most succulent.

But don't do it.

That's right. Though your lobes may be aquiver, all tingly and taut, walk away. No matter how beautiful she is, no matter how crooked her teeth, how bulbous her nose, no matter how willing and submissive she might be, it's *not* worth it.

"Why?" you may ask? Simple. Because let's say you do it, and it goes well. Chances are you're going to want to do it again. And again. And again. And next thing you know, your boss is not only your boss, he's your brother-in-law as well. And that brings us right back to Rule One Hundred Eleven. Forgotten it already? Why do I bother? Hew-mons are hopeless. Okay, I'll repeat it so you don't have to exert yourself by looking it up. "Treat people in your debt like family . . . exploit them." Get it?

Probably not. All I can do is try.

But trust me on this one. Don't ever, under any circumstances, no matter how tempted you might be, forget the One Hundred Twelfth Rule of Acquisition:

"Never have sex with the boss's sister."

Being caught with one's pants down is seldom
conducive to acquiring profit, even on Ferenginar.

"Hamana, hamana, hamana . . ."

R U L E
113

O kay, here's the thing about Rule One Hundred Thirteen, better known as "The Rule that dares not speak its name." The Ferengi are a male-dominated society. The Rules of Acquisition were written by males, for males, and about males. And if that weren't bad enough, let me just remind you. . . . *There are no female bosses on Ferenginar.* And for that matter, no female employees.

I will say no more. The rest is silence.

Thus I record here without further comment the One Hundred Thirteenth Rule of Acquisition:

"Always have sex with the boss."

Yikes.

Ira Steven Behr and Robert Hewitt Wolfe

R U L E

121

In the financial history of Ferenginar, there have been many success stories. But few as impressive as that of Vorp and Sluggo, the creators of that ubiquitous beverage with the happy slimy taste . . . Eelwasser.

Vorp and Sluggo were boyhood friends, boon companions almost since the day their fathers signed the rental agreements on their mothers' wombs. One of their favorite games was stomping around in the Bowog Bog, just a short jaunt from their home in Upper Bowog Bay. Now Vorp, some would say, was short on brains and long on enthusiasm, not to mention slavishly loyal to the smarter, craftier Sluggo. So whenever Sluggo was in need of a good chuckle (and Sluggo loved to laugh), he would convince Vorp to do something funny, like buying air, or talking to females, or eating a few kilos of sand.

Which brings us to that fateful day in the Bowog Bog when Sluggo saw a particularly fetid pool of burbling muck and told Vorp it looked good to drink. The words were hardly out of his mouth before Vorp got down on his hands and knees and started slurping. Sluggo stood and contemplated Vorp's prodigious posterior, which was pointed straight up into the air as Vorp bobbed his head to lap at the muck. But before Sluggo could give his friend's rear a quick kick, Vorp turned back, his mouth slick with slime, and, through algae-stained teeth, uttered those four famous words . . . "Mmmmm. Tastes like eel." And thus, Eelwasser was born.

Soon bottle after bottle of this natural treat was rolling off the assembly line, all featuring the smiling faces of Vorp and Sluggo, pond scum dripping from their chins.

And so it went, for forty years. The two Ferengi bought a huge mansion and lived there with their only companions, a menagerie of albino fangcats (all of whom developed a taste for Eelwasser). People shook their heads in confusion at their unconventional life-style, but one thing was certain. . . . Vorp and Sluggo were friends.

Always remember: Merchandise is your friend
(Terry Farrell).

That is, until Slug-o-Cola.

A consortium of beverage makers, brought to the brink of bankruptcy by the perennial boom market for Eelwasser, finally came up with a new drink that beat Eelwasser in hundreds of clandestine taste tests. But the beverage makers knew they needed a marketing gimmick to overcome Eelwasser's media domination. And so, in one of the most cunning coups in Ferengi business history, they secretly offered Sluggo sixty-five percent of the profits from their new beverage in exchange for being allowed to name it after him. The thought of only *one* algae-stained grin on a beverage label appealed to Sluggo. As he so succinctly put it, "Sixty-five percent beats fifty percent any day."

The rest, as they say, is history. Sluggo moved out of the mansion. Slug-o-Cola grabbed a seventy-one percent share of the beverage market, and Vorp died alone and heartbroken, devoured by a horde of ravenous albino fangcats (which he had grown too despondent to feed).

Vorp had learned a hard lesson. And he ordered it inscribed on his Memorial. So if you ever visit the Bowog Bog, put on your wading boots and slog your way to the Vorp Memorial. There you will find, carved for all to see, Vorp's immortal last words.

Words of wisdom which soon became the One Hundred Twenty-First Rule of Acquisition:

"Everything is for sale. Even friendship."

RULE
# **123**

Fragments from the diary of Rauplop of Rangahorn:

DAY ONE: Today, after long preparation, we have started our descent. The words that Professor Dverl, in his heavy Shploonish Mountain Accent, spoke those many weeks ago still ring in my ears, "Come mit me on a churney to der zenter of Ferenginar!" At least, that's what I think he said. Who can tell with that accent?

DAY FIVE: Still going down.

DAY SIXTEEN: Reached the shore of an underground sea. Built a boat of buoyant pumice stone and set sail. Got violently seasick. Threw up all over Professor Dverl. He shouted something at me which I couldn't understand.

DAY EIGHTEEN: Left sea behind. Found a cave full of never-before-seen wild fungi. Said Professor Dverl, "Behold der myzteriez of der unterverlt!" Took samples.

DAY TWENTY-FOUR: Ate fungi samples. Yummy.

DAY THIRTY: Fungi poisoning subsiding. Feel much better.

DAY FORTY-SIX: Professor Dverl has finally reached a decision. We will take the "looft pazzagevey!" Personally, I would have gone right. But he's the Professor.

DAY FIFTY-ONE: Still hopelessly lost. Professor now claims to have said "richt pazzagevey" but I'm sure he said "looft."

DAY FIFTY-NINE: Where the hell are we? Food running low. Professor going blind.

DAY SEVENTY-FOUR: Stumbled upon skeleton of a large non-Ferengi humanoid. Rotting nametag on underwear said "Saknussen." What could it mean?

DAY EIGHTY-THREE: Professor Dverl, though blind, believes he sees the "glow of licht" coming from one of the many tunnels.

Latinum isn't just a way of life. It's food for avarice.

Maybe he's right. Will wait another day before eating him.

DAY EIGHTY-FOUR: Professor Dverl was right. There was a glow. But it wasn't a way out. It was a vast deposit of pure latinum. I am rich. And very hungry.

DAY NINETY: Professor Dverl picked clean. He vuz goot! Still hungry.

DAY ONE HUNDRED TWENTY THREE: Weak. Starving. Still rich. Haunted by obscure Saknussen reference. Can't go on.

Thus ends the sad tale of Rauplop of Rangahorn. Perhaps you know it from the famous holosuite drama starring Flynk as Professor Dverl and Gormie Gormatop as Rauplop. But trust me, the holodrama's good, but the Rule of Acquisition is even better.

Scribbled under day eighty-five in Rauplop's journal, we see the first mention of the One Hundred Twenty-Third Rule of Acquisition:

"Even a blind man can recognize the glow of latinum."

Okay, time for a little Ferengi language lesson. "Wife" in Ferengi is *booplop*, from *boop*, which means "to serve," and *lop*, which means "one who does a certain thing." "Brother" in Ferengi is *dooplop*, from *doop*, which means "to get," and, of course, *lop*.

So, to Ferengi, there is no more obvious Rule than "*Booplop boop, dooplop doop.*"

Or, in your less poetic human dialect, the One Hundred Thirty-Ninth Rule of Acquisition:

"Wives serve, brothers inherit."

Why is this Ferengi smiling? Three words: Next of Kin.

Ferengi can smell an easy mark a kilometer away.

RULE
#**141**

Don't take this personally, but . . .

Chances are you paid full price for this book. This makes me very happy. This makes Behr and Wolfe very happy. And this makes our publisher especially happy. That's the good news.

The bad news is, it shows once again just how ignorant you hew-mons can be. If only you had looked at this page first. If only you had absorbed its profound wisdom before . . .

Hey . . . come to think of it . . . some of you might not have bought this book yet. Some of you might be reading it in the store. Stop that! What are you? Fatheads? I warned you about this in my last book. No reading in bookstores! Go pay for this right now, then come back and read the rest of this rule.

Okay. Have you paid now?

Yes?

Good.

Read on.

And the next time you buy something, remember the One Hundred Forty-First Rule of Acquisition:

"Only fools pay retail."

RULE
#144

Annual report of the Ferengi Society for the Care and Feeding of Bajoran War Orphans

Submitted for FCA approval
Statement 157-B-878/THX-1138

Gross revenue collected:	117,259,000 sgpl
Expenditures:	
Solicitations:	27,903,000 sgpl
Advertising:	31,822,000 sgpl
Monthly Fund-Raising Dinner 12 months at 121,000 sgpl/month =	1,452,000 sgpl
Royalties Paid on Success's song, "One for the Children and a Dozen for Me," theme song of the FSCFBWO:	9,222,000 sgpl
Office Supplies:	11,035,000 sgpl
Logo Design for T-Shirts:	4,871,000 sgpl
Telethon Expenditures, including rental of Tower of Commerce assembly hall:	17,008,000 sgpl
Salary of Telethon MC, Grymi, lead windsqueezer of Success:	3,500,000 sgpl
Hotel bill for Telethon MC:	1,253,648 sgpl
Misc. Administrative Expenses:	4,957,000 sgpl
Salary of Board Members FSCFBWO:	57,871,000 sgpl
Total Expenditures:	170,894,648 sgpl
Net Profits <or loss>:	<53,635,648 sgpl>
Number of Bajoran Orphans:	235,956

ROBBIE ROBINSON

A Ferengi feeling charitable need look no further
than his own mirror.

Amount of money owed to the FSCFBWO
per War Orphan: 227 sgpl

Figures don't lie. And neither does the One Hundred Forty-
Fourth Rule of Acquisition:

*"There's nothing wrong with charity . . . as long
as it winds up in your pocket."*

R U L E
#162

When my father, Keldar, as you hew-mons would say, "bit the dust," I was bereft. I was still a relatively young Ferengi, and I was concerned that I would not have anyone to instruct me in the finer points of Ferengi philosophy. Then I remembered that my father and latinum were never exactly on a first-name basis, and I didn't feel so bad. After all, I was no worse off without him than I was with him.

Needless to say, I didn't have much hope when it came to the opening of my Legacy Chest, the gift every Ferengi father leaves behind for his son. Sure enough, when I opened the Chest what did I find? Incriminating documents that would allow me to blackmail the Grand Nagus? No. Deeds to tracts of lands containing rich mineral deposits? Not a chance. Star charts indicating the location of the lost latinum mine of Chimera P.? Not even close. A snailosaurus-bone beetle snuff case, hand-carved by the finest Lissepian artisans and encrusted with fabulous jewels and latinum filigree spelling out the name "Keldar?" Yeah, right. My father never even used beetle snuff. So what *did* he leave behind? One word . . . Headskirts. Dozens and dozens of headskirts. And I don't even wear headskirts. Fafa knew that.

My first thought was to throw myself onto the floor and kick and scream until the Blessed Exchequer descended from the Divine Treasury and gave me my heart's desire. So I kicked and I screamed, but no one came. Finally, hoarse and exhausted, I grabbed one of the headskirts to dry my tears.

And then I noticed something. There was writing on that headskirt. "I survived the Bowog Flood!" The Bowog flood? I'd learned about that in school. In 17998, the Bowog Dam mysteriously burst, only days after its warranty expired, and thousands of Ferengi drowned. Had my father really been at Bowog? Then I noticed another skirt, an ancient threadbare garment bearing the motto, "I Stood Tall During the Great Earthquake of 12023!" Soon I realized that all of the skirts bore witness to one great disaster or another: "I Stayed Cool During

At times like this, you have to wonder if there's any profit in, say, the extermination business . . . ?

the Eruption of Mount Tubatuba!" "I Kept Solvent Despite the Financial Collapse of 15799!" "I Dodged the Timber Weevil Stampede! Weevilville, 9183." A cold shiver went down my spine. Could my father have been some kind of foul specter, moving from one disaster to another throughout Ferengi history? Or did he just have bad taste in clothes?

But then it hit me like a head butt from a Klingon. My father was trying to teach me one final lesson. Because each headskirt had a price tag attached. Which meant someone had bought them. And more important, someone had sold them. In the midst of all that suffering and death, someone had been racking their brains to come up with a nice catchy slogan to put on a headskirt.

My father had passed on to me a vivid illustration of the One Hundred Sixty-Second Rule of Acquisition:

"Even in the worst of times, someone makes a profit."

Hew-mons have devils. Ferengi have FCA liquidators.

RULE
#177

It's no secret that the Tholians hate us. They consider us, and I quote, "A foul blight on the face of the universe. A pernicious infestation that must be eliminated." And although we don't have many catchy slogans about it, we don't like them either. But what we do like is Tholian silk. And the Tholians . . . well, they have an absolute mania for Ferengi bog moss. Maybe they eat it. Maybe they line their nests with it. Frankly, we don't know, and we don't care. We just know they can't get enough of the stuff. So the trade routes between Tholis and Ferenginar swarm with ships hauling bog moss one direction and silk the other. It's been this way for centuries. The Tholians claim they will bury us. And maybe one day they will. Or maybe one day the Ferengi will tire of their crystalline insults and launch a vast armada of Marauders to reduce their homeworld to a cinder. (Hey, it could happen.) But in the meantime, I want my suits made of Tholian silk and they can have all the bog moss they want.

After all, the One Hundred Seventy-Seventh Rule of Acquisition clearly states:

"Know your enemies . . . but do business with them always."

RULE
#181

Every Ferengi schoolboy knows the story of Milch the Wanderer. How he traveled the spaceways, meeting primitive aliens and selling them Ferengi beads and trinkets in exchange for. . . well, whatever they had. Who can forget how he purchased the entire planet of Wohoken for a single crate of Ferengi tooth sharpeners? Yes, when it came to shafting the natives, Milch had the magic touch.

Needless to say, Milch was one of Ferenginar's greatest heroes. Even to this day, every Ferengi hopes to make the pilgrimage to Crullus Prime, to climb the Stairs of Gilfoyle, and to stand on the Stone of Deaver, where the Crullers, realizing they'd just sold their entire female population for a fruit basket, finally ended Milch's glorious career (not to mention his life). It's a long journey to Crullus. But it's worth it. Because it was there, on that holy spot, before the flames consumed him, that Milch uttered his famous last words (aside, that is, from "Yooowwwch!").

And my eyes tear and my breast swells with pride as I recall Milch's final defiant cry, as recorded in the One Hundred Eighty-First Rule of Acquisition:

"Not even dishonesty can tarnish the shine of profit."

Hew-mons used to talk about "an honest buck."
Hew-mons are funny.

There's nothing like a little youthful exuberance.

RULE

#**189**

TO: CADET FIRST CLASS NOG
    STARFLEET ACADEMY
    PIKE HALL, ROOM 714
    SAN FRANCISCO, CA94II6SF89II
    NORTH AMERICAN ADMINISTRATIVE DISTRICT
    EARTH, SECTOR OOI
    UNITED FEDERATION OF PLANETS

Dear Nog,

Just heard the news from your father. I have to admit, I was more than a little concerned that attending Starfleet Academy would dull your instincts for profit. But to find out that you've been implicated as the leader of a dom-jot gambling ring among the cadets. . . . I am SO PROUD.

Now Rom seems to think that you're concerned about how this might affect your Starfleet career. I hope he has as usual misread the situation. But on the slim chance you may actually be a bit worried . . . let me put things in perspective. Sure, you may have lost some status among the other cadets. And, yes, this incident will undoubtedly go down on your permanent record. And perhaps in some not-so-far-distant future, human-o-centric powers-that-be may use this as an excuse to prevent you from achieving that Captaincy you have your heart set on. But believe me when I tell you . . . It's worth it.

At least, I certainly hope it was worth it. I'm told you can make a lot of money hustling dom-jot. If you need investment counseling, you know who to call.

> Your loving uncle,
> Quark

That nephew of mine may have been corrupted by Federation values, but at least he apparently still remembers the One Hundred Eighty-Ninth Rule of Acquisition:

> *"Let others keep their reputation . . .*
> *you keep their latinum."*

Business with a Klingon invariably involves a minor
misunderstanding or two along the way.

RULE
#192

More correspondence from my files:

TO: KALAW, SON OF LORKA
        C/O KALAW'S KLINGON KITCHEN
        THE PROMENADE, LEVEL I, SECTION D
        DEEP SPACE 9

FROM: QUARK, SON OF KELDAR
        PROPRIETOR, QUARK'S BAR AND GRILL (ETC.)
        THE PROMENADE, LEVEL I, SECTION A
        DEEP SPACE 9

RE: LOST PROPERTY

Kalaw, I have searched high and low throughout the bar, and I still cannot find the jeweled Klingon dagger that you allege to have lost in my establishment. I feel compelled to remind you of our strict "no liability" policy in regard to such circumstances. If you wish to avoid such incidents in the future, I suggest you refrain from carrying such expensive items with you when you go out drinking. You might also consider not imbibing quite so much bloodwine. You were unconscious for at least two hours before I was able to convince Morn to carry you home. Personally, I prefer to be awake when I'm around Morn, but he was the only one strong enough for the job. Rest assured, however, that if the dagger shows up, you will be the first to know.

TO: STOL, SON OF PROMP
        STOL'S HOUSE OF COLLECTIBLES
        1515 SPLORPLOP CIRCLE
        MEYUPYUP DISTRICT
        ROPLERMOOP CITY RCII 98C F29
        FERENGINAR

FROM: QUARK, SON OF KELDAR
        PROPRIETOR, QUARK'S BAR AND GRILLE (ETC.)
        THE PROMENADE, LEVEL I, SECTION A
        DEEP SPACE 9

RE: NEW MERCHANDISE

Cousin! All sorts of good stuff for you this week. Five Bajoran earrings, one combadge, a tricorder, a gross of self-sealing stem bolts, and best of all . . . a genuine jeweled Klingon dagger. And the best part is, it's in perfect condition! It was owned by a chef, and he never used it for anything except cutting gagh! The jewels alone must be worth a dozen strips of latinum. I await your offer.

Best,

Quark

P.S. Still keeping an eye out for those Jem'Hadar breastplates you're looking for. I'll let you know.

There's nothing quite so satisfying as the proper application of the One Hundred Ninety-Second Rule of Acquisition:

"Never cheat a Klingon . . . unless you can get away with it."

RULE
#194

riends, now that you've almost finished reading *The Legends of the Ferengi*, I'm sure you're eager to pay Quark's a personal visit. In order to better serve you when you arrive, please complete the following form, and send it to:

QUARK'S
c/o Starbase Deep Space 9
Bajor Sector, Alpha Quadrant

You'll be glad you did.

NAME:_____

SPECIES:_____

OCCUPATION:_____

EXPECTED DATES OF VISIT:_____

FAVORITE FOOD:_____

FAVORITE DRINK:_____

ON A SCALE OF 1 TO 10 (10 BEING HIGHEST) HOW MUCH DO YOU LIKE:

GAMBLING:_____

DABO GIRLS:_____

FAMILY-STYLE HOLOSUITE PROGRAMS:_____

ADULT-STYLE HOLOSUITE PROGRAMS:_____

WOULD YOU BE INTERESTED IN ANY OF THE FOLLOWING GUIDED TOURS? (mark Y/N)

A PROMENADE SHOPPING EXCURSION:	Y	N
A ROMANTIC DINNER IN AN UPPER DOCKING PYLON:	Y	N
ADVENTURE TOUR OF THE OLD CARDASSIAN ORE PROCESSORS:	Y	N
SPELUNKERS' PARADISE: (crawlways, conduits, Jefferies Tubes)	Y	N

A Ferengi loves to welcome new customers, especially
if he can charge admission.

WEEKEND GETAWAY TO BAJOR:	Y	N
SKI TRIP TO BREEN:	Y	N
A TRIP THROUGH THE WORMHOLE:	Y	N
(please complete accompanying liability waivers)		

WHICH OF THE FOLLOWING ADJECTIVES BEST DESCRIBE
YOU? (Circle all that apply.)

Good-natured	Forgiving	Happy-go-lucky
Rich	Incredibly rich	Private moon owner

Casual drinker	Serious drinker	Klingon
Suspicious	Paranoid	Cardassian
Naive	Jaded	Generous
Thrifty	Trusting	Ferengi-friendly

WHAT BEST DESCRIBES YOUR RELATIONSHIP WITH FERENGI:

Never met	Met once or twice	Done business with
Victimized by	Cheated by	Befriended by
Like	Dislike	Hate with genocidal fury

PREFERRED FORM OF MONETARY EXCHANGE:_____

GROSS ANNUAL SALARY: _____

Thank you in advance for your help. We can't wait to see you here at Quark's . . . the friendliest place in the galaxy. And remember, order a Black Hole and get a free commemorative mug for only five slips of latinum.

As you can see, I'm a firm believer in the One Hundred Ninety-Fourth Rule of Acquisition:

"It's always good business to know your customers before they walk in the door."

RULE
#**203**

In my life, I have only met two people who've actually written a Rule of Acquisition. One was Grand Nagus Zek, leader of the Ferengi Alliance and the greatest business mind in the Alpha Quadrant. The other was Stumpy Strope, restaurateur, bartender extraordinaire, philosopher, and friend. I met him while I was a ship's cook on a Ferengi trader, tramping around the galaxy seeking my fortune. He owned a watering hole on the frontier world of Roughlanding. We used to stop there every two months to pick up supplies. I always looked forward to those visits, and the happy times at Stumpy's Bar. I'd stay after closing, and we'd drink long into the night. It was Stumpy who taught me how to mix my first Black Hole, to run a dabo wheel, and to short-change even the most vigilant customers. But one thing we never talked about was Stumpy's right leg . . . or lack thereof. He didn't seem to want to discuss it, and I didn't press.

But then came my final visit. I'd signed the lease for Quark's, and I wanted to pay my respects before saying goodbye to Roughlanding forever. Stumpy and I had a hell of a time that night. Black Holes, Flaming Novas, bloodwine . . . we drank it all. And by the dawn, even Stumpy's ears seemed to be weaving unsteadily. And that's when I finally got up the courage——to ask the big question, "Stumpy? How'd you get the name Stumpy?"

He looked at me for a long time. His eyes seemed to mist over, as if recalling a great sorrow. And then, he said to me, "Quarkie," (he always called me "Quarkie") "You're a fine Ferengi lad, so I have to believe you know your Rules of Acquisition."

"I do," I replied proudly, not sure where this was going.

"So you know Rule two oh three?"

"Like my own name," I said, desperately trying to recall my own name.

He leaned over the bar, propping himself up on his one good leg, then tilted his head close to mine. Our noses were almost touching. And when he spoke, it was with the fire of righteous-

Caution: Gouging customers may sometimes
work both ways.

ness and one too many Flaming Novas. Just before I passed out
from the fumes, this is what I heard. . . .

"Rule Two oh Three. I wrote it."

And as my consciousness faded, I finally remembered what
I like to call "Stumpy's Rule," the Two Hundred Third Rule of
Acquisition:

*"New customers are like razor-toothed greeworms.
They can be succulent, but sometimes they bite back."*

Let the other guy clean up. You count the latinum.

R U L E
211

You'll find it in every Ferengi business establishment, both on Ferenginar and off-world. Sometimes it's written large across the walls; other times it's subtly tucked away in some obscure corner. But believe me, it's there. It's always there. Fifteen little words that form the foundation of the Ferengi business ethos. Try to make profit without them, and you are doomed to fail. Remember them, and everything is possible.

Honor these fifteen little words. After all, they're the Two Hundred Eleventh Rule of Acquisition:

"Employees are the rungs on the ladder of success. Don't hesitate to step on them."

Damn good advice.

R U L E
#214

As you know, previously we've discussed such tasty Ferengi eatables as tube grubs, greeworms, Slug-o-Cola, Eelwasser, slug steaks. . . . Wait a minute. . . . What's that blank look on your face? Have you been skipping around in this book? That is totally unacceptable. This tome was written to be read cover to cover, preferably in one sitting. Or if you prefer, to be kept in your waste extraction unit and savored, one rule at a time (or two, depending on how long you're in there). You're not supposed to browse through it, like it's some random collection of musings. A lot of thought went into this. It's a mosaic, with each piece building on the one that came before. Now go back and start from the beginning.

There. Done? Good. Now, you definitely know about tube grubs, greeworms, Slug-o-Cola, Eelwasser, and slug steaks. But without a doubt, the single most popular foodstuff on Ferenginar is ChiggerBurgers™. There used to be a saying that you couldn't walk a block on Ferenginar without passing a ChiggerBurger Emporium™. That is, until people came to realize there were ChiggerBurger Emporiums™ every half-block. You may ask, why do we like ChiggerBurgers™ so much? Well, for one thing, "They're the Krunchiest burgers in the Galaxy!"™ But the other reason we like them is because we have no choice. ChiggerBurgerCorp has seen to that. Ever since old man Logi opened his first ChiggerBurger™ stand back in 14305, the company has been known for its aggressive advertising and marketing strategy. Back then there were few Ferengi who would dare pass Logi's stand without purchasing at least one ChiggerBurger™. Rumor has it that those who refused ended up being ingredients instead of customers. But over the years ChiggerBurgerCorp became more sophisticated in their sales approach. They do the usual subliminal advertising in holosuite dramas. They manufacture genetically engineered insects that whisper "ChiggerBurgers™ . . . Good" into your ear. They spell out their corporate logo on roadways. But their true stroke of genius is Mandatory Direct Marketing.

Beware of finicky eaters; they generally make
poor business partners.

MDM works like this. Every morning, in billions of homes throughout the Ferengi Alliance, ChiggerBurger™ salesmen arrive at the door carrying your daily supply of ChiggerBurgers™. Your bank account is duly debited. Now to be fair, no one stands there making sure you eat your ChiggerBurgers™. But you have to pay for it whether you eat it or not. So most people go along with the program and consume at least one ChiggerBurger™ a day. Every day of their lives. That's what I call advertising.

So, as I sit here munching on a ChiggerBurger™, washed down with an extra large Slug-o-Cola, I give you the Two Hundred Fourteenth Rule of Acquisition:

> *"Never begin a business negotiation on an*
> *empty stomach."*

If you don't like it, take it up with ChiggerBurgerCorp. It's their Rule.

R U L E

IN MY PREVIOUS TOME, *THE FERENGI RULES OF ACQUISITION*,
THIS RULE WAS MISLABELED AS RULE #117. THE TRUTH IS,
IT'S RULE #217. DEAL WITH IT.

Of all the folktales of Ferenginar, and there are a lot of
them, probably the most enduring is "The Story of Ving
and Ding." Over the millennia, their tale has been
turned into several dozen plays, countless auditory sculptures,
one thousand seven hundred fifteen holosuite dramas, and two
hundred twelve songs (including ballads, limericks, and the
megaband Success's hit recording, "Ving and Ding and Their
Special Thing").

Not to mention one very profound Rule of Acquisition.

The story in a nutshell is this:

Ving and Ding were brothers whose parents were travelling
across the Blopfep Wilds. In the middle of their journey, their
parents were killed by a freak flash flood (or a herd of rampaging
snailosauri, or the evil Smiling Partner, or they just died of old
age, depending on who's telling the story). Anyway, poor little
Ving and Ding were left to fend for themselves. Luckily, they
were taken in by a pack of giant timber weevils who raised the
children as if they were their own. The boys learned to burrow
for grubs, suck the sap out of jooble roots, chew through hooyup
trees, and bang rocks together (why giant timber weevils like to
bang rocks together no one knows). The brothers would spend
hours peacefully pulling spiny thorns out of each others'
hindquarters with their teeth, fully believing that they were just
a pair of shell-less, four-limbed, mandibly challenged timber
weevils.

And then one day, when they were eleven (or seventeen, or
forty-two, depending on who you believe), a friendly Ferengi real
estate developer tore down the entire Blopfep Wilds to put up a
discount shopping area called Weevilville. The timber weevils
were hunted down, stuffed, and sold as souvenirs. But one of the

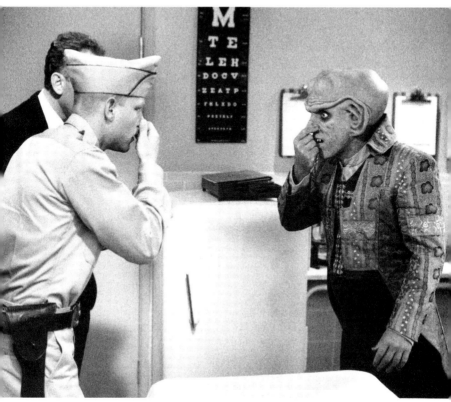

Monkeying with primitives (James G. MacDonald) may
be good for a few laughs, but the gains are almost
always short-term.

hunters found Ving and Ding, and to quote Success, "took them
under his wing. Ving, Ding, under wing, la-la-la, yeah, yeah,
yeah." (I love that song.)

Under the tutelage of the hunter (Success called him Fing,
but I think they made that up), Ving and Ding soon became
productive members of Ferengi society. A talent agent for the
Pilum Porous Agency heard their amazing story, and before they
knew it, Ving and Ding were travelling all over Ferenginar doing
their weevil tricks for appreciative, well-paying audiences.

It is said that during their one year of touring, Ving and Ding made more profit than the Grand Nagus himself. (To which Fing the Hunter replied, "Why not? They had a better year than he did.") But then, to everyone's surprise, they vanished. At first it was thought that foul play was involved, that perhaps they had been kidnapped by the jealous Grand Nagus. But no ransom note appeared and no bodies were ever found. Their disappearance became the greatest mystery of its time. Ferenginar swarmed with amateur Ving and Ding sleuths, seeking high and low for the lost lads (and hoping to be handsomely rewarded by Pilum Porous, Inc.).

But years went by, and gradually Ferenginar lost interest in the brothers. Only Fing the Hunter continued the search. For fifty years, he sought them, from the sleet-covered streets of Rangahorn to the fetid jungles of Hoopoohoopoo. And then, one day, in the forests of Loom, Fing came upon a pack of giant timber weevils. And leading the pack were the two grimiest, spine-riddled timber weevils of them all . . . Ding and Ving. Hard as it may be to believe, the brothers had thrown away their fame, their glory, and their profits to return to the simple life of their boyhood. When Fing saw the brothers (now full grown alpha-male timber weevils), he approached them with tears of joy in his eyes. But Ving and Ding descended on him, banging rocks together like all good timber weevils do. Unfortunately, in this case, they made sure that Fing's head was between the rocks. Poor, sweet Fing.

When he heard about this story (don't ask me how, since Fing was dead and Ving and Ding were off weevilling in the wilderness), Blemin the Bard wrote the first of many dramatizations about the boys, "The Strange and True Tragedy of Ving and Ding, the Timber Boys," or "Once a Weevil. . . ."

As was his habit, Blemin attached a clever moral to the end of the play, and that moral became the Two Hundred Seventeenth Rule of Acquisition:

"You can't free a fish from water."

He was deep, that Blemin.

RULE
#223

Remember the Barter Age? Not like you were there, because that'd mean you were very, very old. I mean, do you remember our last story about the Barter Age? Rule Twenty-Two ring a bell? Commerce Zones, feuds, bloodshed, and all that nasty stuff? (I don't want to be a pest about this, but you'd get so much more enjoyment from this book if you didn't skip around so much.) Anyway, picture yourself back in the Barter Age. To be more specific, in the village of Kope on the warlike Plains of Plol. Got it? Good. Now for our story.

One day, the noted sage, Yinkee the Shrewd, was indulging himself at the Happy Lobes Inn, a place well known for its potent fermented snail juice and its lithesome, scandalously clothed females. Yinkee had just finished his seventh snail juice and was eyeing a particularly dextrous lass (wearing feathered gloves up to her shoulders!), when DaiMon Yomgro, the village's Security Consultant, burst into the tavern.

Yomgro seemed upset, to say the least. According to him, an army from the neighboring Commerce Zone was on its way to Kope. Yomgro ordered all the males to leave at once and prepare for battle.

As hard as this may be to believe, back then Ferengi actually valued courage in battle more than cunning at the negotiating table. But at least the males of Kope had their priorities straight. They agreed to fight, but only once they'd had their fill of hard spirits and soft *oo-mox.*

But Yomgro protested. "There's no time!" he insisted. "Put down those females and pick up your cudgels! For the hour of truth is at hand!"

Yomgro must've been a very persuasive speaker, or the females weren't as lithesome as everyone said, because the Ferengi males actually did as they were told. They turned their backs on *oo-mox* and strode forward, heads held high, and cudgels held even higher, to meet the enemy. . . .

All except for Yinkee. His appetite was as great as his

They have a saying on Risa: "What is ours is yours."
Who are Ferengi to argue?

wisdom, and he looked around at all the unimbibed snail juice and all those available females, and realized where he was truly needed. So he tarried behind, telling himself he'd leave for the battle as soon as he'd finished his business at the Happy Lobe.

Fifteen hours later, head swimming in snail juice and lobes happily numb, Yinkee staggered onto the battlefield, only to find it littered with bodies. Yomgro had led the men of Kope to their deaths. Yinkee sighed, "That could be me lying there, all chopped up." But then he smiled and let out a contented belch. *Oo-mox* and snail juice had saved his life.

Yinkee lived to a ripe old age, and told his story so often that it became the basis of the Two Hundred Twenty-Third Rule of Acquisition:

"Beware the man who doesn't make time for oo-mox.*"*

RULE
#229

The greatest sculptor in the history of Ferenginar was Meelo the Mold Master, of the city of Glunge. You may have seen his famous statue "Lonz and his Nose Flute" which still stands in the Glunge Marketplace today. But Meelo's greatest work was his statue of Voshma the Voluptuous. This life-size representation of a naked Ferengi female was so breathtakingly beautiful that it was said no male could look upon it and not fall hopelessly in love. Maybe it was the perfectly carved nose, maybe it was the delicate lobes . . . or maybe it was just the fact that she was made of solid gold-pressed latinum.

But if Voshma had many admirers, none was purer in his devotion than Meelo himself. He was so smitten with his work that he would spend hours each day polishing it, buffing it to a high sheen, so that even after ten years, Voshma glowed as brightly as when she was first cast. Some say Meelo even spoke to the lifelike statue, that he treated it in every way as if it were his own wife. Let's just say that for those ten years, Meelo got very little work done.

But one day, a strange thing happened. As he was contemplating Voshma's perfect golden hindquarters, Meelo heard a buzzing sound in his workshop. "Open your palm," a tiny voice whispered. Confused, Meelo did as he was told. To his amazement, a small creature landed on his open hand. The creature looked like a teeny, tiny, itsy-bitsy Ferengi with wings. "I am Znip, the spirit of love" the creature said. "And few on ferenginar love as strongly as you do. Such devotion deserves reward."

Now this sounded good to Meelo. After all, no Ferengi ever turned down a reward. "What did you have in mind?" Meelo asked.

Znip smiled. "You adore Voshma, but your love is wasted on cold hard latinum. I will make Voshma a real ferengi female, so that your passion can be consummated and your love made real."

Now Meelo was a quick thinker. He did some quick calculations. And he came to a quick conclusion.

Brief moments of ecstacy with your female (Mary
Crosby) can't compare to the enduring joy of profit.

"Thanks," he said, "but no thanks."

And with that Meelo brought his hands together with a thun-
derous clap that could be heard clear across the city of Glunge.
And znip was no more.

Meelo wiped his hands on his pants and went back to
contemplating the golden beauty that was Voshma.

Though I'm sure he was sorely tempted, Meelo was obviously
a firm believer in the Two Hundred Twenty-Ninth Rule of
Acquisition:

"Latinum lasts longer than lust."

RULE
#236

17,882 was a very interesting year on Ferenginar. In that year alone, over twenty thousand Grand Nagi held office; the Ferengi Financial Exchange crashed 3152 times, while setting 12,322 record highs; there were 41,098 civil wars; an unknown number of Ferengi incited interstellar wars (estimates are in the millions); and the Ferengi sun went nova at least once a week. In other words, 17,882 was the year Ferenginar discovered time travel.

Imagine the confusion. Ferengi from all over the Alliance were rocketing backwards around the sun, visiting the Guardian of Forever, diving into black holes, and generally making a temporal nuisance of themselves. It was the best of times and the worst of times, sometimes all at the same time.

Think about it. Some young ambitious Ferengi hears about the whole time-travel craze and gets a hold of a few hundred thousand chroniton particles. Now maybe he goes into the future, to figure out how the market will act so he can anticipate it in the past . . . or maybe he goes back into the past, to change history, so that his investments will be more valuable . . . or maybe he does both. Or tries to do both and does neither. Or does one of them three times and one of them twice. Temporal dynamics is a bitch. But whatever he chooses, there's a good chance he'll wind up killing his own grandfather, marrying his own grandmother, accidentally causing the extinction of every tube grub on Ferenginar, preventing the invention of the wheel, and basically creating a temporal mess too horrible to contemplate.

And he wouldn't be alone. Because in 17,882, it seemed like everyone had their own personal timeline.

Something had to be done.

And a bold Ferengi named Twim did it. Just how he did it is anyone's guess. Some say he came from the distant future to impose his temporal tyranny on Ferenginar. Others say he was just a gambler from the suburbs of Noi, who built his own time

It's been said that time is the fire in which we burn. Ferengi
know time is just a pain in the lobes.

---

machine and went back to the beginnings of the universe itself to stack the deck in his favor. Whatever he did, it worked. When the dust cleared, Twim was the Grand Nagus, and the penalty for time travel was death.

Now I know what you're thinking. You could be like Twim. You could travel through time, rearranging history to your liking. But don't try it. You'll only get in trouble. And frankly, things are confusing enough as they are.

So leave time travelling to the professionals, and remember Twim's Rule, the Two Hundred Thirty-Sixth Rule of Acquisition:

"You can't buy fate."

And remember, it's not just a Rule. . . . It's the law.

R U L E
239

I know what you're thinking. You're almost done with this book, and it's beginning to sink in that the title *Legends of the Ferengi* doesn't tell the whole story. Sure, there are legends. Plenty of legends. But there are also songs, FCA reports, auction notices, an obituary, a school paper, not to mention carefully selected memos from my files. Now some of you may think that a book entitled *Legends of the Ferengi* should consist of legends and nothing but LEGENDS. You might accept a myth or two, but in your opinion, anything else reeks of betrayal.

You couldn't be further from the truth.

What you have in your hands is a veritable potpourri of Ferengi culture, a wealth of information never before seen by hew-mon eyes. It's ridiculous to think I didn't have enough Ferengi legends to fill up a book. The Ferengi culture is a rich and ancient one, with tens of thousands of years of written and oral tradition. I wasn't being lazy. I didn't do things this way to reduce my workload. The bottom line is *this book was specifically designed to meet your needs.* Customer satisfaction was my highest priority.

And besides, even if *Legends of the Ferengi* isn't entirely accurate, it is a catchy title. And catchy titles sell books.

Which is why I chose to follow the Two Hundred Thirty-Ninth Rule of Acquisition:

> *"Never be afraid to mislabel a product."*

It doesn't matter what a thing is. All that
counts is what you call it.

R U L E
#242

One of the most prestigious schools on Ferenginar is the Haryalevard Academy of Business Management. Among its graduates have been seven Grand Nagi, twelve Chief Liquidators of the FCA, and Ferenginar's only military dictator, DaiMon Vurp, also known as Vurp the Inevitable (r. 15791–15792). Its first headmaster, the Venerable Chig, was the most honored scholar in Ferengi history. It was Chig who said those immortal words, "There are no stupid boys on Ferenginar. All right . . . maybe one or two."

Haryalevard is also by far the most profitable school in the Ferengi Alliance. Some believe this is because of the outrageously high tuition. True, the average Ferengi must go into debt for seventeen to eighteen years to pay for a Haryalevard education. But where the Academy really rakes it in . . . is the Student Store.

Now, we're not just talking notebooks and styluses, severely overpriced and sold to a captive audience. Surprisingly, that accounts for only a fraction of the Student Store profits. No, the real money is in souvenirs. Because even if you didn't go to Haryalevard, you can still make people *think* you went to Haryalevard. All you need is a desk plaque . . . or a banner . . . or a headskirt, or any other knickknack embossed with the Academy's coat of arms. And where can you get those and approximately two hundred fifty other signature items? The Student Store, of course.

Now, you might say to yourself, I could buy a blank headskirt and write the word Haryalevard on it. I could even use the school colors (mauve and taupe). And you could. But you'd be making a mistake. Because Haryalevard has graduated seven Grand Nagi. And 7,899,023 litigators. And all the best ones work for . . . the Haryalevard Academy Student Store. Can you say, "Copyright infringement"? They can.

So let's take a moment and tip a glass to my alma mater. (And I've got a banner hanging in my bar to prove it.) To her moss-covered walls and soggy octangles. Long may she thrive.

Here's another hew-mon proverb: "You can't have everything." It's a wonder they made it off the planet with that kind of attitude.

And let's never forget the school motto, emblazoned on the Academy's hallowed Toll Gate and recorded as the Two Hundred Forty-Second Rule of Acquisition:

"More is good . . . all is better."

A good marriage should be profitable for both parties.

RULE
*#*255

T he following article appeared on the front page of the *Ferengi Acquirer* on Glorpober fifth, 18,083.

GOUGE-MINING MAGNATE ESCAPES DEATH
WIFE CHARGED IN MURDER ATTEMPT

In the early morning hours, latinum mining king Squeeb, son of Been, was hauled from the flaming wreckage of his skimmer by two members of his private medical staff. Though suffering from various injuries, Squeeb is expected to make a full recovery.

Shortly after his rescue, FCA liquidators arrested the victim's wife, Jubbletta, and charged her with attempted murder. It seems Jubbletta had struck her husband over the head with a bar of latinum, stuffed his unconscious body into his skimmer, and then programmed its autopilot to crash into one of Squeeb's own gouge mines.

Luckily, unbeknownst to his wife, Squeeb has a duridium plate in his head, an unwanted souvenir from his stint in the military during the Lytasian Conflict. This plate cushioned the blow, enabling Squeeb to regain consciousness at the last moment and seize control of the skimmer, causing a fiery, but not fatal accident.

Initial reports indicating that Jubbletta was having an affair with Squeeb's accountant, Vinx, and was conspiring with him to take over Squeeb's financial empire seem to be in error. Vinx was questioned by Liquidators, but released on Squeeb's request. No charges have been filed against the accountant.

Read between the lines, and you'll see that duridium plate or no duridium plate, Squeeb was a shrewd businessman.

Because even in a crisis, he didn't forget the Two Hundred Fifty-Fifth Rule of Acquisition:

"A wife is a luxury . . . a smart accountant a necessity."

RULE
#261

It's said something strange happened to Squeeb, the latinum mining king, after his brush with death (see Rule #255). Beyond all logic, he came to appreciate life more than latinum. He began to spend his days wandering about the countryside, smelling the bog flowers, watching the suns set. Obviously, the man was deeply ill. But before he could seek professional help, fate, in the form of a holodocumentary he was watching, dealt him a cruel hand. The program detailed the plight of Ferengi gouge miners. Now in the hierarchy of Ferengi jobs, gouge mining is third from the bottom. It's only one step above waste-extraction technician. And two above the worst job on the entire planet, which frankly I don't even have the stomach to describe, but you know if it's worse than being a W.E.T., it's pretty bad.

Anyway, gouge mining isn't much fun. The hours are bad, the pay is low, and the workers have a life expectancy only slightly longer than a Tellurian gnat. Since Squeeb employed approximately one third of all the gouge miners on Ferenginar, he took the holodocumentary very seriously. But instead of suing the holomakers for libel like any sane Ferengi, Squeeb actually started worrying about his workers. He even got the twisted idea that he was somehow responsible for their plight.

Lost in his madness, Squeeb decided to see for himself how his miners lived. Traveling to one of his largest gouge mines, he personally donned a pair of protective lobe shields and descended into the sweltering hot mine. There he revealed his presence to the miners and announced that he wanted to hear any grievances they might have against him.

It's said that by the time the miners were through with him, all that was left of Squeeb was the battered duridium plate that once lined his skull.

So let's have a moment of silence for poor confused Squeeb.

No Ferengi ever got rich feeling guilty.

And while we're at it, how about we dedicate the Two Hundred Sixty-First Rule of Acquisition to his memory:

"A wealthy man can afford anything except a conscience."

See what happens when you forget your Rules?

R U L E
#263

Of all the Ferengi success stories, none is less likely than that of Oblix, son of Sner. Oblix had no lobes for business. He couldn't add, couldn't subtract, and couldn't remember any of the Rules of Acquisition.

But he could talk.

And talk, and talk, and talk. It's said he could outtalk a Cardassian and still have energy left to debate logic with a Vulcan. And the strange thing is, people liked to listen to him. In no time at all, Oblix became the greatest motivational speaker in the history of Ferenginar.

Oblix's seminars, often held in tropical resort locations, became required listening for top executives from all over the Alliance. It's said people came from as far away as Romulus to listen to Oblix's rousing speeches, filled with business advice, market tips, and investment strategies. So persuasive was he that a whole generation of Ferengi adopted his philosophy of business.

Ironically, no one can really explain what that philosophy was. When his speeches are analyzed, they appear to be vacuous and somewhat ephemeral, filled with vague examples and irrelevant stories. Bombastic in style and void of content, Oblix seems to have hit on a magic formula . . . talk and keep talking until anyone who doubts your words gives up from sheer exhaustion.

Never was so much said about so little to so many. And never was so much admission charged to hear someone say so much about so little to so many. Oblix quickly became one of the richest Ferengi of his time, continuing his fiery (and very profitable) orations until he died an untimely, but well-deserved death from a ruptured vocal cord.

We honor his memory. He sold nothing to everyone and got away with it. Truly, he was the perfect Ferengi.

Interestingly, when boiled down, Oblix's eighty thousand hours of recorded speeches can be summarized perfectly by the Two Hundred Sixty-Third Rule of Acquisition:

"Never allow doubt to tarnish your lust for latinum."

Of course, he said it a lot louder.

R U L E
#266

This book was intended as a public service, a way to help you pathetic hew-mons achieve your true profit potential (which admittedly in most of your cases isn't much, but hey . . . you gotta try). And in the spirit of service, I thought it might be a good idea, as we draw to a close, to provide some specific examples of what to do when your misuse of these Rules leads you astray. In other words, in business, as in life, it always pays to have a really good lie ready for emergencies. Here are a few of the best:

"Your payment is en route by subspace transfer."

"When I mentioned that profit figure, I clearly stated that it was only an estimate."

"I have no independent recollection of those events."

"I am not a crook."

"Ear massages are commonly exchanged during Ferengi business negotiations."

"I left it on that table over there. Some Vulcan must've taken it."

"Quark? Never heard of him."

"Ferengi are renowned throughout the Alpha Quadrant for their honesty and integrity."

"The warranty is provided by the manufacturer. If you contact him, I'm sure he'll be happy to give you a complete refund."

"I already gave you your change."

And my personal favorite:

"It's my brother Rom's fault."

Try them out. Once you see how well they work, you'll never tell the truth again.

KIM GOTTLIEB-WALKER

Truth in business is like matter and antimatter: If you
put them together, they blow up in your face.

And never forget the Two Hundred Sixty-Sixth Rule of
Acquisition:

"When in doubt, lie."

If there really is such a thing as a "cosmic truth,"
it exists in Rule #284.

RULE
#284

Well, you're almost there. Just a few more pages to go. But before you finish this book, close the cover and put it on your shelf in a place of honor, walk over to the nearest mirror. Hold the book up to the mirror. Now look at yourself holding the book in the mirror. This book that you have just purchased and read. Ask yourself . . . why did you buy it? Oh, sure, the book is clever, hilarious, and erudite, and it makes a great gift. But we both know that's not why you shelled out your hard-earned latinum for your very own copy.

No. You wanted something more valuable. You wanted wisdom. You wanted the inside knowledge that have made the Ferengi a force to be reckoned with in the business world. In other words . . . an edge on the competition. You want that edge. You need that edge.

Yeah, yeah. I know what you're going to tell me. You're a hew-mon. You're better than us Ferengi. You've evolved "beyond greed." Well I say to you . . . study that figure in the mirror, the one clutching a copy of this book. Look at yourself.

Look long and hard.

And you'll come to realize that you, too, are living proof of the Two Hundred Eighty-Fourth Rule of Acquisition:

"Deep down, everyone's a Ferengi."

RULE
#285

One last letter from my personal files, with a lesson for all of us.

To my beloved Publisher,

I note that as of today, it has been two months since my book <u>Legends of the Ferengi</u> was published on Ferenginar. I'd like to remind you that I advised against publishing this book on my homeworld. I specifically stated that this was a book intended solely for the hew-mon market. I am sure you recall our extensive conversations on the subject. However, you are the publisher. . . . I'm merely the lowly writer. You won, I lost. Fine.

Except for one problem. It's been two months and I'M STILL IN JAIL! What's the matter with you people? You're a highly respected publishing house. I would think you'd have some highly respected lawyers on your payroll. Now maybe they've all been on vacation for the past two months. Maybe they're all busy taking care of other authors incarcerated because of your bad business decisions. But, frankly, I'm not interested in excuses. JUST GET ME OUT OF HERE!

I wrote this book as a public service. I was trying to facilitate a better understanding between hew-mon and Ferengi. Is that so wrong? Do I deserve to rot here for the rest of my life just for telling a few stories? All right, so I forgot to pay the copyright fees to the descendants of Lonz Golden Nostrils for quoting his song "The Wind in My Ears." And perhaps it was rash of me to imply that the Ferengi Skimmerway Construction Department was a pawn of the Slug-o-Cola Bottling Company. And I probably crossed the line when I said, in jest, that ChiggerBurgerCorp might be overly zealous in its advertising campaigns. But it was all in good fun. No one was harmed. And any instances of libel, slander, copyright infringement, or illegalities of any kind were purely unintentional.

I'm sure a deal can be arranged. It'll just take a little effort on your part. And I have faith in you. I know that you're not just

letting me sit in jail to cheat me out of my royalty payments.
You're too evolved for that. Too noble. I know it's just an oversight,
and your lawyers will be attending to my case shortly. I'll be out
of here in no time . . . Right? Right?

Yours in innocence,

Quark, Son of Keldar, aka Prisoner #17-237-991

I never thought it would happen to me, but it did. I stand
before you, an unfortunate and undeniable example of the Two
Hundred Eighty-Fifth Rule of Acquisition:

"No good deed ever goes unpunished."

ACKNOWLEDGMENTS

Ira Steven Behr and Robert Hewitt Wolfe would like to thank the following people, without whose love, affection, and attention, this book would've been finished a lot sooner: Laura Behr, Roxanne and Jesse Behr, and Celeste Wolfe.

We'd also like to thank the writers, staff, cast and crew at STAR TREK: DEEP SPACE NINE, above all Jill Sherwin who spent hours proofing this manuskript.

Finally, we'd like to pay special tribute to all the actors whose willingness to don a bulbous rubber head gives life to the Ferengi, most especially:

Max Grodénchik
Aron Eisenberg
Wallace Shawn
Jeffrey Combs

and
(trumpet fanfare, please)
the Quarkmeister himself:
Armin Shimerman

We love you guys.